Love, Dirt

Iowa Short Fiction Award

Love, Dirt

Bruce Johnson

University of Iowa Press · Iowa City

University of Iowa Press, Iowa City 52242

uipress.uiowa.edu

Cover design by Kathleen Lynch
Interior design and typesetting by Sara T. Sauers
Printed on acid-free paper

Library of Congress Cataloging-in-Publication Data
Names: Johnson, Bruce, 1986– author
Title: Love, Dirt / Bruce Johnson.
Description: Iowa City: University of Iowa Press, 2025. |
Identifiers: LCCN 2025007520 (print) |
LCCN 2025007521 (ebook) |
ISBN 9781685970390 paperback |
ISBN 9781685970406 ebook
Subjects: LCGFT: Short stories
Classification: LCC PS3610.O32364 L68 2025 (print) |
LCC PS3610.O32364 (ebook) |
DDC 813/.6—dc23/eng/20250418
LC record available at https://lccn.loc.gov/2025007520
LC ebook record available at https://lccn.loc.gov/2025007521

For my father

Contents

The Knack

I ONCE HAD A FRIEND who could tell you where you were from. This was a hell of a trick for social gatherings. She'd be in the corner, sipping something with gin in it, and I'd be beside her drinking beer. Inevitably someone would approach. This was Las Vegas, the best place for this trick, a city nearly no one was from.

Cheryl worked with me at a small PR firm that handled several clients on the Strip. Like most men in PR in Las Vegas, I was gay. I am still gay, obviously, though I say "was" because I am no longer friends with Cheryl, no longer work at that tiny little firm. But back then I loved this trick of hers, to watch it rankle people. I spent all my time on the Strip, even lived there, in a small studio apartment on the fourteenth floor of the Cosmopolitan. I took most of my meals at buffets or trendy burger cafés, watching the yard-high margaritas go by in the arms of women who were all leg or men all muscle. As a rule, I preferred people in my life to be only passing through.

The people on the Strip enjoyed her talent the way you enjoy a magic trick, an enjoyment mixed with stubborn confusion and an annoyance that there are things in the world you do not understand. We would have these club openings or these red carpets or these media whatever-the-hells and people (mostly men) would approach and want to talk to her. This was their "in." She was beautiful, I suppose, in the boring sort of way straight men seem to be drawn to. I was happy to observe this fray from the outside.

Is it true? they would say. Let's see it.

Cheryl would sip up the last of her drink and hand them her empty glass. Get me another, she would say, then I'll do it for you.

This was an essential part, she told me. She could only do the trick if she had a fresh drink nearby. She was somehow always right at the end of a drink.

When she got the new drink she'd remove the straw and take a long, thoughtful gulp. Cheryl was one for theatrics, and it was hard to see where the performance ended and the real knack began. She would usually shut her eyes. Then she'd put a finger to her temple, rubbing in small, circular motions. Or she'd fold her hands as if in silent prayer, or rock back and forth on a stool if she was sitting down. A pained expression would darken her face, a downward tilt to her features. I was the only one who knew this expression for what it was, an earnest effort not to smile.

Say something, she'd say. Let me hear you speak.

She'd listen intently as the men rattled off whatever came to mind. Usually empty details: their name, their position, the make and model of their car. Sometimes some cheesy line about how she looked that night.

Okay, she'd say, shut up. You're from Kalamazoo.

Or: Poughkeepsie, New York. Hopkinton, Rhode Island. Chubbuck, Idaho. Grand Forks, North Dakota.

Sometimes she'd get angry. Chicago, are you kidding me? Give me a real challenge.

People had their theories, of course. Some thought it was an accent game, that she had an incredible ear for regional accents then just played the numbers. It wasn't that she *never* got it wrong, after all, just rarely—sometimes she'd tell you that you were from a town you spent a lot of time in as a child, as if something essential from that place had rubbed off on you. Other people figured she spent time scouring the internet, studying public records. It couldn't be that hard to find this info if one really tried. Half of everyone had their hometown up on Facebook anyway. It wasn't inconceivable that she found this information for people she was likely to run into at media functions.

Others thought it was a trick of psychology, that everyone somehow betrayed this info in the way they responded to her question. Like when you ask someone a math question: If they look up, they're a visual learner. Sideways means aural, downward kinesthetic. Maybe if you say "Speak to me" and someone scratches their eyelid, they're from Poughkeepsie. If they pull their lower lip, Grand Forks.

I begged her to tell me how she did it. She never would.

Though fewer, there were women too who were interested in her gift. Most seemed to genuinely enjoy the trick, as an impressive talent that didn't need to be put on trial. But there were occasionally women who were more standoffish around Cheryl, as if they were only there to see what all the fuss was about. The beginnings of their questions were tentative, often needling: "So, you're the one they say can." Or, "I've heard you've got a good trick." These women seemed to think there was something distasteful, even cheap in Cheryl's knack, its invasiveness.

Once, near the end of Cheryl's time in Vegas, an important man named Stilson Dodd asked Cheryl where he was from. Dodd owned one of the flagship steakhouses on the Strip. Cheryl and I were sitting on stools by the bar on the rooftop of a casino when he approached, celebrating a new lucrative concert space.

So, Dodd said. They say you can tell me where I'm from.

Cheryl nodded, and shut her eyes. She knew better than to ask Dodd to get her a drink. She told him to start talking, and Dodd began to describe the stools at the bar of his steakhouse. Hand-sewn Italian leather. Exotic wood.

That's enough, Cheryl said, opening her eyes. You're from New York, New York.

Dodd turned red. His nostrils flared. How dare you, he said.

He looked at me. You in on this? he asked. I held up my hands as if in surrender.

You listen to me, Dodd said to Cheryl, finger in her face. My mother was only there six months. New York was the worst time of her life, of both our lives. Just because I was born there doesn't mean I am from there.

I think that's exactly what that means, Cheryl said quietly. Or maybe you misunderstood your own question.

Dodd took the drink from Cheryl's hand, the drink some man had gotten her, and threw it in her face. Then he handed me the glass and walked away. I looked over at Cheryl.

I didn't know real-life people threw drinks, she said, bewildered and dripping.

I handed her a cocktail napkin from the bar. Maybe it's a New York thing, I said.

After that, Cheryl didn't like to do her trick. She'd seen how the wrong bit of biography could unsettle someone, and decided it wasn't worth the headache. She told me in a voice where I couldn't tell if she was joking that that's why she left where she was from, anyway: too many people with too many drinks, too many people who threw things.

So now people would come up and ask her and she'd say no no no, that's someone else you're thinking of. Or no no, I don't do that anymore.

Some people would press, though, usually important people: prestigious chefs, owners of nightclubs, managers of departments or sometimes entire properties. People who loved to hear things about themselves. People who loved to make her do what they asked of her.

To these people Cheryl had little recourse. They were powerful, these people. Her job was PR, after all, which mostly meant building relationships, and snubbing them would be bad for business. So she'd say, reluctantly, Okay then: Talk to me.

Something had changed, though, by then. Cheryl seemed incapable of her old knack, that simple geographical placement. But she had to say something, so she'd shut her eyes. There would be a moment where her face was perfectly calm, serene even, and she seemed not to know where she was. In these moments she'd speak in spite of herself.

You're from a big empty house, quiet and deathlike—like a museum after closing time, or a long-abandoned tomb.

Or, You're from a place that gets very cold at night, and you were always terrified to ask for another blanket.

You're from that comment your father made once, the one about if you'd never been born.

You're from the folders your father kept hidden in his desk drawer. You're from the secret language you made with your sister, the one you only pretended to understand. You're from all the places your mother never took you. You're from San Jose, California, that summer your brother drowned.

Cheryl quickly became an industry pariah. Anger trumps amazement, and this new phase of her knack angered people. These events were often packed, the context for these revelations public. These were things people didn't want to hear anywhere, especially not in front of friends and coworkers. *That's not funny* was the most common response, by people convinced Cheryl was playing a cruel trick. It was clear that the most she could hope for in Vegas was to tread water. She wasn't long for the world of the Strip, the world of PR.

The man who had started the trouble, the Not New Yorker Stilson Dodd, took me aside at another rooftop party one evening. One of our clients, the Cupcake Factory, had provided cupcakes for the gathering.

Dodd said he saw great things for me, or at least good things, if I knew how to associate with the right people. Before we rejoined the others, we shook hands in that businesslike way, the way where you try to match the other's firmness, a perfect pitch of pressure. Cheryl was waiting in a corner, alone. Someone had asked me earlier how I knew her and I told them the truth: I didn't remember. For the life of me, I could not remember meeting her or ever deciding to be her friend. We worked at the same PR firm, so I guess that was that. And I was amused by her little trick. Being from Las Vegas myself, I was always interested to see where others flocked from.

She glared at me when I joined her in the corner. She'd seen me talking to Dodd. She was on an action plan by then, to correct her sub-satisfactory performance at the firm. She'd made too many enemies, when her job was to make friends. Within a few weeks, she'd be gone.

I asked why she was glaring at me like that. Why she couldn't keep her eyes smiling, her words kind. There was a drink in my hand all of a sudden, and I began to take sensibly sized sips. When she didn't answer, I asked her if she remembered how we had met, or why we had become friends. I told her I could not remember. She shook her head.

Then I asked her where I was from. I knew I had probably mentioned at some point I was from Vegas, but I wanted a more nuanced answer, like the answers she'd been giving lately. She shut her eyes and her features went smooth. How unsettling it must be, I thought, to find your best moments of calm in thinking about other people. She told me to start talking. I told her about the shirt I was wearing, and started to count the buttons.

I want to say you're from nowhere, she said, but that isn't quite right. It's more like you're from everywhere, all at once. You're from the high heels your mother had, the back of her calves. All the people who ever smiled at you, just because. Your father's cuff links, the way he never wore them but still periodically took them in to be shined. The princess movies you loved as a child. The girlie mags you hid beneath your mattress, in case anyone ever checked. The way whenever anyone asked your mother she said "Catholic," though you never once saw her go to Mass. And the time you skipped school to see how far you could walk in one direction before someone came and found you, then called home from a payphone when no one ever did.

She said it was hard to explain, but it was like everything in me added up to zero. The way atoms seem solid to the touch when they're mostly just empty space, particles held to loose orbit by contrary charge. She said that appearance of being solid was why I was destined for above-average things.

I nodded, still sipping. And you? I asked. Where are you from?

I said it because it seemed like the thing to say. I don't remember her response.

On the way out, I helped her carry the leftover cupcakes to her car. We placed them in the back seat. They would be a gift for the break room, for all the worker bees. But instead she forgot them in her car overnight, and in the morning when she got outside the Vegas heat had melted them all together, a mound of frosted mush. She put it in the break room as a joke. The people there ate it with spoons.

In Case I Don't Call

WHEN THEY WERE YOUNG, Michelle and her little brother shared a phone line in the basement. Their parents got it for them because Michelle insisted, since it seemed all the other girls in her grade had their own lines. And her parents obliged, because really there was no better argument Michelle could have chosen—in all matters of parenting, they deferred to what they took to be popular opinion.

The only one to object was Alan. He was five years younger than she was, and he hated having to "field her calls," as he put it, hated having sole responsibility to write down his big sister's messages. But what was worse, the thing that really got him yelling, was that so many of Michelle's friends mistook him for her. His voice hadn't changed yet, and countless times Michelle came home to a yellow Post-it stuck to the receiver, a scribbled name and number and an angry command: *Tell your friend I do not sound like a girl!!!*

Now Alan wore a red dress and light makeup, rouge on the cheeks, a thin layer of lipstick that matched the polish on his nails. He served her steak from a cast-iron skillet, bloody, on an old ceramic hand-me-down plate from their childhood. Baked potato on the side, sour cream and chopped chives. In the center of the table, a bowl of salad topped with shredded carrot for color. The women's clothes were something new, a thing of the last six months or so. His features were naturally feminine, something she had always been jealous of. Model-skinny, high cheekbones, pouty lips and long lashes. Though he wore makeup, he didn't need much.

"I almost made a wine reduction," he said. "But I remembered you like it plain."

He set an open bottle of red down in front of her. The table, small and round and crammed into the corner of the kitchen, was just big enough for the two of them.

She nodded. "Wine's for drinking," she said. She poured herself a glass.

Last week when he called Michelle to invite her to a homemade meal at the small house he rented, she'd silently ticked off all the possible reasons in her head—he wanted to borrow money, he needed help moving, he had some message for her to relay to Mom and Dad. Once he'd invited her over under similar circumstances to sell her knives, some Cutco knockoff he'd started working for and shot all his money into. Or maybe he had some crazy news to share, a sudden elopement perhaps.

"I want to ask you for something" was all he'd tell her on the phone.

"Yeah, I figured."

"You may not like it."

"I figured that, too."

Things weren't always easy between them. An age difference of five years was an eternity in child-time. Her little brother, her *baby* brother.

When she was in middle school she railed against her parents when they made her let him tag along with her, and made him pay with the sort of verbal barbs only an elder sibling can deliver. When he was still years away from being called "fag" or "queer" by kids his own age, she started to make fun of his skinniness, his hair, the effeminate lilt to his voice and walk. She made sure every one of her friends knew all the most embarrassing moments from his life so they could make him relive them—the time he had to be dragged from the theater when he started crying at the start of *Finding Nemo*, or when he wet the bed for fear of the ghost she told him haunted the bathroom at night.

She was mortified now to think of all this, all the hard times she'd given him. By the time she reached high school she'd become fiercely protective of him to compensate and remained so on into adulthood. When his ex-boyfriend recently ran around on him, Michelle concocted a whole list of revenges Alan made her swear not to carry out—slashing the man's tires, egging his house, using the key Alan still had to get inside and sell the man's best possessions on eBay. But she and Alan still fought often; every time he called she had to think for a moment whether she needed to act mad when she picked up. And she always picked up.

Now she sat and ate while Alan made conversation to avoid asking her whatever he wanted to ask. She tried to remember if she'd ever seen him set out cloth napkins before, if she'd even known he owned any. They talked about her new job, corrections officer at the medium-security-level jail in Kearney, a job she'd moved two hours away for, away from Lincoln where they'd always lived. They talked about his new job at a home improvement store, getting things off high shelves and assembling various pieces of furniture. He complained they wouldn't let him wear earrings. He was twenty-two now; she was twenty-seven. They both had half a college degree. His major had been theatre, while hers remained forever undeclared. She wanted to tell him he should go back to school, but it seemed hypocritical. Anyway, she reminded herself, he was a grown man now. It wasn't her place to worry. He got enough of that from their folks.

"Is this what you wanted to talk to me about?" Michelle asked. "Your new job?"

"No, of course not," he said. "At least not exactly." But he did not elaborate.

After dinner he put her plate, fork, and knife in the sink with a squirt of soap and a thin layer of bubbly water. She followed him to the living room and sat down beside him on the couch. He crossed his legs at the knee and turned toward her. His legs were smooth. She felt her cheeks grow warm when she wondered how much of his body he had shaved.

"So?" she said.

"So. I have a business proposition."

"Then the answer is no. Last time you borrowed money it took you three times as long as you said to pay me back."

He narrowed his lipsticked lips, confused. "Last time I borrowed money I was seventeen," he said.

"Still."

He shook his head. "You don't need to put in any money. I'm going to pay you. All I need is for you to check in on me. You work security now, right? I want you to work security for me. Earn a little extra cash on the weekends."

He said, "I'm going to be meeting some men."

He explained her role first, in simple, logistical terms. She began to understand some of her responsibilities and flashes of what she would be doing, with no real grasp of the overall situation or what he was planning to do. Who were these men? They didn't sound like friends.

He said he would make a point to have it happen in Lincoln, and she could be at his house if she wanted, watching TV, eating Fritos, sipping beer. She would have her nightstick—they gave her a nightstick at Kearney, didn't they? And all she had to do was have her phone on. He would tell her what time he would call, and he would call. Nothing to it.

If he didn't call, though—which he would, he stressed he always would, ninety-nine point nine nine percent—then she'd have the address where he'd be. She could come check up on him, extricating him if he needed to be extricated.

"Extricated," she repeated.

"It means get me the fuck out of there."

"I know what it means," she snapped. "But I don't understand. Who are these men you're meeting? Why are you afraid? Are you in trouble?"

"I'm not afraid. I'm cautious. I meet them online."

"So they're dates."

He opened his mouth then seemed to think better of it and shut it again. He laughed a nervous laugh that reminded her of their mother and strafed his eyes toward the kitchen, the sink filled with tepid water and dirty dishes.

"I guess you could say that," he said.

She looked away, hoping she had misunderstood his meaning.

"I'll pay you well," he was saying now, as if that were the issue. "What do you make at Kearney? I'll pay you that, or a little more, if you want. I'm sure you can use some extra cash."

She shut her eyes, literally shut her eyes, so she did not have to look at him looking at her. "Where do you meet these men?" she asked.

"Online. There are plenty of sites."

She opened her eyes. Her brother had that cowed look like when he used to get yelled at as a child, or beaten up at school.

"To think when Mom calls I tell her you're doing well."

"I *am* doing well, thank you. Though I'm surprised she asks."

"They'll lend you money."

"I don't want their money. I don't want anything they have."

"What do you want, then? What is it we didn't give you?"

She wanted to say *Why can't you just be normal?* but stopped herself, ashamed. Michelle often resented her own slide into normalcy, the slide that seemed inescapable now in her mid-twenties, as if she were a grain of sand filing with all the others toward the funnel of an upright hourglass. She'd moved two hours away for the job at Kearney, not because she was passionate about law (far from it, in fact) but because jobs for dropouts were hard to find and the money wasn't bad. It was the sort of work a sixteen-year-old version of herself would have made fun of, blowing smoke from a joint out the car window, snarking about all the jerkoffs who worked for the prison system. Now she couldn't smoke weed, her job drug tested. The people she met in Kearney were the small-town types good for a beer and some sports talk and little else, and most of the time she spent her evenings at home, having a Budweiser and a Hungry-Man TV dinner in front of some sitcom.

As for her question—what is it we didn't give you—she knew it was ridiculous. Their father understood little past the year 2000. A daughter who took another girl to prom, not because she liked girls but just to piss people off. A son who started crying on the third day of flag football practice when he was made to run laps with grass-stained knees. At the dining room table their father complained of having to explain these things to his friends, the other workers at the plant, saying things like *You know Jimmy's boy, he's about to skip a grade* or *Tim's girl's on the pep squad at* her *school, how 'bout that.* Instead he was stuck with two children who always got good grades but constantly cut class, then dropped out of college—an offense he took as a personal affront to all the opportunity afforded them by the long hours he'd worked over the years. And then their mother, who never had anything to say, who faced the world with a perpetual look of silent disapproval, who when her husband badgered their son about why he never had any girlfriends and asked one day in a half-joking but fearful tone if Alan was "queer or what," just turned her head and said, "Stop it, Roger, you'll make me sick."

She wanted to ask her brother: What more could *I* have done? What more could you and I have done for each other? She felt her anger flare. *But we turned out all right* is how she ended every story she told about her childhood, on the rare occasions she did talk about it. She so wanted that to be true.

Alan generously ignored her question. "I know people who have done it here and there," he said. "It sounds no less pleasant than stocking shelves."

"It's illegal."

"My sister the saint."

"It's dangerous," she said.

"Not if I have you checking in on me," he said. He took a clove cigarette from a pack sitting on the coffee table and offered her one. She took it, though she didn't normally smoke. She needed something to do with her mouth that wasn't scold.

He lit hers, then his own. He tugged absently at the hem of his dress. "You've been checking up on me my whole life," he said. "Making sure I was okay. Might as well get paid for it, right?"

Prostitution was a thing she was not exactly against, not in theory. She was not one to tell women or men for that matter what they could or could not do with their bodies. She'd heard stories of the way it was in Europe, state-regulated brothels, everything clean and safe and on the up-and-up. That seemed fine. But she knew women here who'd done it, she'd met them at Kearney, awaiting trial in their tiny cells. These women's lives were shot through with heartache and missed opportunity. Whether they were the ones out in the yard, lifting weights and getting in fights over everything from tampons to mobile phones, or the ones who rarely left their cells and looked so skinny they might squeeze through the bars, they all carried with them an air of hopelessness that reminded her eerily of her mother.

"If you want to talk about it," she said, "we can talk about it. But I'll tell you right now, one hundred percent, I will not do it. I can't control you but I don't have to support you. I won't do it."

"Fine," he said. He took one last long drag of his cigarette and stabbed it out in the ashtray. "But I will tell you, then, *one hundred percent*"—a mocking tone here, the voice they used to use to mimic their mother—"I'm going to do it, whether you help or not. I only wanted to give you the opportunity to help make it safe. I can find someone else. I just asked you because you're the biggest badass I know."

She tried hard not to be flattered. She was a "bulky" woman, that was her mother's favorite word for her, in those moments that made her wish that she, like her brother, no longer talked to her parents. When she was in the fifth grade and had been called fat by one of the more popular girls, Trish McKinley, she'd handled it the only way she knew how: She beat the shit out of her. And she wasn't fat, not really. Her bulk was all muscle. A brief suspension and a stint of counseling appointments later, and she was free of those schoolyard taunts forever.

It was, she'd realized with a stab of unease years later, not far from the jail yard rules she'd heard batted around Kearney: Pick a fight the first day and win, then everyone will know not to mess with you. Here, too, she saw the line between criminal behavior and normal behavior grow fingernail thin.

"I know people who have done it," Alan said again. "Turned tricks."

She could tell he enjoyed saying this phrase, the kitsch of it.

"I do too," she said. "They're in jail."

It wasn't that he needed the money, he told her, at least not in the way she thought. He had a job, thirty hours a week, the maximum they could give him without offering benefits. He made rent and paid bills okay, had money budgeted to go out drinking one night a week. It was the kind of average, comfortable existence she could see terrified him to think could stretch out for another forty-five years until retirement. He didn't want this measured life where he had just enough to scrape by and even build up his savings if he really scrimped, but no money to travel and no vacation time to take even if he did come by the money.

He seemed to counter her counterarguments before she said them, speaking in the matter-of-fact way people gave PowerPoint presentations in offices on TV. He had no delusions of glamour—he wanted to make that clear. He had those friends who did it, and they'd told him stories. The clients were mostly overweight or elderly. They had eczema patches and wheezing breath, or some hard-to-pin-down mental handicap. Once one had an oxygen tank with tubes clipped to his nose, the occasional hiss of escaping air. But time with Oxygen Tank Man would lead easily to sharp new dresses, a flat-screen TV. Lifting a few fat rolls to get at what was underneath was nights out on the town, a fund for early (and more comfortable) retirement. In one hour he could make what he made in a full day of work. Which of the two was more demeaning, then? Besides, he said, these people needed people like him. Elderly people paid for all sorts of companionship—that was natural.

"Listen," he said, frowning down at a place on his thumb where the polish was chipped, "I don't want what you have. What you and Mom and Dad have." He took a big red gulp now straight from the wine bottle, all decorum dissolved, and wiped his mouth with the back of his hand. "I don't want our parents' lives," he said.

She had all sorts of things she wanted to say to this, meant to explain if not excuse their parents' shortcomings while acknowledging how difficult things were for her and (mostly) for her brother. That it was not their parents' fault, not entirely, that the world they were raised in was drastically different than the world now, the perceived needs (or lack thereof) of children a world away.

Instead she said, "I am *nothing* like our fucking parents."

What followed was her dismissal from his house, after the volume and pettiness of their conversation gradually rose until they were shouting at each other, culminating in a slammed door with her on the other side of it. Alan had told her that, on the contrary, she was exactly like their parents. Old-fashioned prudishness, a stubborn insistence on the value of hard work and the American dream, and worst of all the judgment, the unsolicited advice about everything from what job to take to what men to date. And Michelle had called him lazy, a fuckup, someone sure to end up in a jail cell somewhere fermenting fruit in the water tank of a state-owned toilet. A woman in bifocals watched curiously out the window of a neighboring house until she saw Michelle looking and darted her head back inside.

The first call he made was an angry voicemail he left on her phone before she even got out of Lincoln. It cajoled her for being a bad sister and homophobic to boot, daring to tell him what rights he had to do what he would with his own body. The next one, another call she silenced, came right as she pulled up to her house in Kearney. "I'm sorry," the voicemail said simply. The voice was tired, ragged, torn up from tears and cigarette smoke. "Please call."

She waited a couple days to respond, as long as she dared. She wanted to wait longer. She had perfected a kind of artistry in protracted silences. Silences that conveyed anger at first, then sadness, and eventual indifference. It was then that whomever she was feuding with would cave. Her mother calling to apologize for whatever comment she had made about her weight, some friend who'd stiffed her on borrowed money, a lover who had made eyes at one of her friends. With Alan it had always been that he'd had some emotional outburst, and he'd call to laugh and say maybe he was on the rag, a joke that offended her mildly but she always let go because she was relieved to hear his voice again.

But this time she had no such opportunity. She had issue with her brother's scheme for a variety of reasons—its legal concerns, its ethical implications, what people would think of him (and her, she had to admit she worried about how having an occasional prostitute for a brother would reflect on her)—but the part that made her finally pick up the phone, a breathless feeling of pride-be-damned panic pounding at the inside walls of her chest cavity, was that she worried for his physical well-being. Her kid brother was beanpole thin, sexy in a dress, feminine in all the worst ways. This was only one in a long string of what she considered bad sexual decisions—he was always going for the biggest, gruffest man he could get his hands on, then acting shocked when he was mistreated. He needed to be protected—he had that part right at least. So she sat in her spare living room in Kearney, picking at a hole in the upholstery of her secondhand couch, and dialed him up.

There was a pause when he picked up and she heard him puff at a cigarette.

"You shouldn't smoke," she said, wishing now he hadn't seen her do so just a couple days before.

"That's the strangest start to an apology I ever heard," he said. "I've got a date tonight. This might not be the best time to talk."

"A date?" she asked. "What type of date?"

He laughed. "The old-fashioned kind. Not business, pleasure. Hopefully not *too* old-fashioned, you know."

"And the other thing?"

"I'm still waiting for you to say yes."

That was good. She had hoped he would say that. She'd thought about it and finally decided that she'd known her brother long enough to know she wasn't going to change his mind with words.

So she took a deep breath and said what she'd planned to say, just as she'd planned to say it: "All right, then, let's talk money." And after arguing for a higher price long enough to convince him she was serious—*Come on, Alan, this is illegal, you've got to pay more than my day job*—Alan told her to be in town the following Saturday and they hung up.

She had an old pair of handcuffs in her glove box she intended to use. She took them out in her brother's parking lot and tested the key several times, watched them clasp and unclasp, then shoved them in her back pocket. One of her exes had left them at her house. He had thought they could use them in the bedroom and she had laughed in his face. It was just the sort of thing Alan would make a joke about, handcuffs in the bedroom—he loved the sort of risqué jokes you could tell at parties, those jokes that made her uncomfortable in a way she couldn't explain.

She knew she couldn't police her little brother, not anymore, not really. But if he was going to revert to childishness, to acting out, to shortsighted behavior with no nods to adult responsibility, then she was going to treat him like she did as a kid. Physical restraint, maybe a good punch or two. She'd make sure he missed his "date." She hadn't punched him in over a decade, and she was sure it would hurt much more now. She had a sense that this was what he wanted, had always wanted. Why else would he have told his big sister his plan? He had to have known her reaction in advance.

He was in his living room putzing about nervously when she arrived, which he stopped just long enough to let her in and set a bottle of wine and a glass on the table for her, along with a bottle of mineral water. He gestured to the old tube TV in the corner, said if the remote didn't work at first just smack it a couple times. It was after dark and the end table lamp that lit the room had a light bulb out, so her eyes had to adjust. He started to explain everything to her, how he'd write down the address of where he'd be, it wasn't far, fifteen minutes away max. He'd call promptly at 10:00; if it turned 10:01 and he hadn't called then she needed to come get him immediately, but whatever happened just stay calm. This was perfectly safe, all just a precaution. He wore a pair of sharp black jeans and a silk sport shirt. She hadn't seen him this dressed up since high school graduation.

He cracked his knuckles nervously and wiped his palms on the back of his pants. He laughed that twittery laugh that again reminded her of their mother, but this time it was a bit higher, like he was trying to do an impression of his normal laugh but couldn't hit the right pitch. "Jesus," he said. "I'm nervous!"

She stood between him and the door. She crossed her arms.

"Do you need anything else?" he asked, motioning at the water, the wine.

"You'd better sit down," she said. She stood as tall and straight as she could, feet slightly apart, as broad-shouldered and doorway-blocking as she could be. "You had to have known I wouldn't let you do this."

"You've changed your mind?" She could tell by his tone that he was annoyed. "Because we've been over this. With you here, there's nothing to worry about. Oldest profession in the world—isn't that what they say?"

"You want me to protect you," she said, "I'm here to protect you. Sit down." She stepped forward and put her hand on the back of his neck, a pressure somewhere between motherly and hostile. She tried to maneuver him gently toward the couch.

He knocked her arm off. "Hey. Cut it out."

"Don't be a child," she said. "Sit down."

He shook his head. "Forget it," he said. "I shouldn't have asked you. I thought it might make you feel better, doing the security thing. Keeping me safe. It was for your benefit, not mine."

He tried to step around her and she sidestepped into his path.

"Sit down," she said.

"Come on." He tried to dart around her and she shoved him up against the wall. His head slammed and he stumbled, almost fell. "Jesus," he said, and she saw his eyes flick to the glimmer of the handcuffs as she pulled them from her back pocket.

He stepped backward, farther into the room, and put a hand to the back of his head to check for blood. She felt a flare of satisfaction at this. He hadn't hit his head that hard.

"In case you forgot," he said, his eyes now steadying on hers, "you are not a real cop. You only handle people who are already behind bars."

When Alan was young, he'd become briefly obsessed with wrestling after his parents gave him a used Nintendo system that came with a WCW game. He'd spend hours on the thing trying different holds, mashing the buttons until the lettering wore away. Then he'd hand a controller to Michelle and try to teach her to pull off some new move he'd discovered, shouting "Up B! Up B!" until, laughing, she'd set the controller aside and lift him up and throw him down playfully in her best imitation of a body slam.

These were the moments she thought of when she stepped forward to grab him, to wrestle him to the ground and pin him there as she cuffed him. She paused mid-step, though, as she realized she wasn't exactly sure how to do that. How was she supposed to hold both his hands still and buckle the cuffs as well? And restrain him too? She cursed herself for not watching a couple YouTube videos of cops doing this before she came.

While she was deliberating, Alan stepped forward and—in a move all too reminiscent of that old wrestling game—put his leg behind hers and shoved her to the ground. She'd never been struck by him, not as an adult, and even with what she was trying to do she hadn't expected it. It seemed impossible, even as it happened, little Alan toppling her to the ground. She landed on her back and felt the wind rush out of her, and an eye-watering pain started to spread across the back of her head.

Breathless, stunned, she started to lift her head but it was too late. She saw a blur of feet speed past her, and Alan slamming out the screen door.

At 9:50 she was sitting on Alan's couch, ice pack wrapped in a dish towel pressed to the back of her head, watching the muted news. The lump was the size of a small marble, warm and tight beneath her hair, and the ice didn't seem to be helping. She sipped a cup of tea, trying to stay alert, trying not to keep looking at her phone. She had resigned herself to waiting until ten, to make sure he called. She hadn't decided yet what she'd do when he returned.

She'd tried to run after him, out the front door, once she regained her breath. But he was gone, car screeching out the driveway and up the street. A few minutes later his text came through. *I'm about to walk in!* it said, as if nothing at all had transpired between them. *Wish me luck! I scheduled another message to come your way at 10:01 with the address of where I am, in case I don't call. I'm putting this on silent, so don't bother responding.*

At 9:55 she did what she had told herself she wouldn't do—she cracked open the wine bottle. She wanted to stay alert but her nerves were fluttering so she took a drink, then another, and started to pace. She knew it would be 10 on the dot when he called, or close to it. He'd told her the man was paying hourly, that after all this trouble he was still on the clock.

Glaring at the phone on the table, she realized that there was a part of her, small but swelling larger, that she had previously refused to recognize. A part of her that did not want the phone to ring.

No, she wanted to be right. She wanted to be the one to show up at the supplied address, to drag the other man (pervert!) from his house by the hair and slam his head to the pavement, to beat his face to a bloody mess with the nightstick she'd refused to use on Alan.

At 9:59, the phone rang. A cheery but embarrassed brother, saying everything went fine and that he was on his way now. He asked if she was still there. "Of course," she said, blood pounding in her ears, her eyes threatening tears, a war cry stifled in her throat. "Of course I'm still here."

Love, Dirt

CHARLES DARWIN HATED it here. On the same voyage that would later take him to the Galápagos Islands, where the abundant wildlife inspired his theory of natural selection, he was first forced by a winter storm to seek shelter on Chiloé, a Chilean island off the southern coast. He remarked in his diary on the island's gloom and ceaseless rain, saying the climate made it "a miserable hole."

My father is from here, as he's happy to tell anyone who will listen. He and my grandparents moved to Nevada right before the Chilean coup, in 1972, but he is always recounting his memories of Chiloé, possibly embellished over the decades—loitering outside the Castro bus station to hear the news of unrest on the mainland, watching his friend's father chop through the forests' dense shrubs and centuries-old evergreen trees, trading tales of ghosts ships and the warlocks who secretly ruled the island. He bought me an illustrated book of chilote myths when I was a kid, placing an international call to the printing press in Valdivia for them to ship us a copy.

In 2005, I'm sixteen and in Chiloé for the first time. My parents and I are staying by an unnamed beach in an old house my father is helping his friend Yaco fix up and turn into a bed and breakfast. It's the first time they've seen each other since they were six. Back then Yaco's father worked for my grandfather, commuting in his beat-up truck twice a week to Castro to tend Grandpa's yard and perform whatever odd jobs were needed—installing new tile, replacing light bulbs, whatever. In the summers Yaco would tag along, and he and Dad would play outside until dark fell and Yaco had to head back to his home out in the country.

After they moved, my father begged and pleaded to send letters to Yaco, but my grandfather told him that any letter Yaco's family might receive—as unlikely as it was to make it to Chiloé in the first place—could spell trouble. There were rumors of disappearances in Chile after the coup, people blindfolded and sequestered in the night. A letter from abroad could be taken the wrong way, as some sort of socialist code. Knowing my grandfather, I suspect that along with any concerns about the safety of Yaco's family was a distaste for the idea of Dad continuing to mingle with the gardener's family. In any case, after the dictatorship ended in 1990 (and after all the worst rumors about the disappearances had proven true), my father and Yaco rekindled their friendship through the unreliable postal service between the two continents, their letters sometimes taking months to arrive.

All this is exceedingly present to me as in the upstairs bedroom of the bed and breakfast I slide my hand eagerly down the pants of Yaco's fifteen-year-old son and at the same time hear the front door unlatch and swing open. Mateo is already hard. It's the first dick I've ever felt and I keep hold for a long, desperate moment, refusing to believe I have to let it go, though I know the sound from downstairs means my parents are back early. Mateo shoves me in the chest and I see sheer terror scrawled on his face. I have not come out to my own parents, but from his expression it is clear that whatever consequences I fear are nothing compared to what getting caught would mean for him. My father warned me on the flight here: the island is isolated, rural, cut off from the rest of Chile. Some areas are still without electricity, and people like it that way. He said not to even mention the word "dictadura"—they don't all see it that way.

I jump up from the bed and adjust my jeans—throbbing, nauseous. I hear footsteps. We are both still visibly aroused and probably reek of weed. Instinctually I pull Mateo by the hand toward the giant wardrobe on the opposite side of the room. We both scrunch inside, old winter coats dangling around us and boots clustered around our feet. We angle our bodies away from each other and listen.

I am filled with fear but thrilled to be trapped so close to Mateo. He is whispering something in Spanish I don't quite catch, then I realize he's praying.

Mateo and I are supposed to be clearing out the attic, dragging the old boxes wet with mold down to the junk heap on the side of the house, making sure none of them hold anything of value. This is our punishment for the night before, when our parents caught us sneaking gulps of chicha from the jarras in Yaco's kitchen. The adults are supposed to be in the nearby village, having a decadent lunch and spending the day in town while we settle for day-old empanadas. We had only gone through one box, full of buttons, thread, and old sheets of fabric, when Mateo asked in shy Spanish if I smoked pot and produced a joint rolled in a Bible page from his shirt pocket. His slender fingers were barely bigger than the joint.

We smoked on the back deck, balancing carefully on the few boards that weren't rotted through, creaking and bowing underfoot. This had been his great uncle's house, who had moved to Viña del Mar decades earlier to sell overpriced boat rides to tourists and never bothered to tell anyone the house was still in the family. Recently he'd died and left it to Yaco. My father was lending time and money. I asked Mateo if he thought our dads would really get this place fixed up well enough for a bed and breakfast and he shrugged, took a deep puff, and passed the joint to me.

He said, in Spanish, Please, with these chilotes? My dad probably just wanted an excuse to invite yours here. No way they don't put more into this than they get out of it.

My father would have been delighted to hear himself called a chilote, even after so many years.

We smoked fast, knowing we only had so much time before the colihuachos found us, massive black bugs at their worst that time of summer—a type of fly but unlike any fly I'd ever seen, aggressive and big as paddle balls. I'd only been in Chiloé a few days and had already gotten used to them, though I'd been warned they could bite. Later I'd read online that, like all large flies, colihuachos feed on mammalian blood to produce their eggs, and when they make love the act begins in the air and ends in the dirt.

One buzzed up into Mateo's face as we smoked and he tried to burn it with the plump glowing cherry but missed and almost fell through a rotting board. I put out my arm and he grabbed it, the most natural motion in the world. He held on just a beat longer than necessary. I took the joint from him and tried to puff at it naturally, as if I weren't relishing the white marks his fingers left on my forearm even as they faded.

Inside, we flopped onto the bed in the master bedroom, the only decent piece of furniture in the house. It was bought in Castro, on clearance, and hauled there in the back of Yaco's truck with my father's help our first day on the island. A single wood nightstand sat to the left, covered in white water rings, and in the corner was a ratty old wood wardrobe that I knew had to weigh a thousand pounds and would be a pain to get down the stairs. There was also a small picture tube TV, the only one in the house, sitting on a flimsy tray table. It wasn't hooked up and I can't imagine it worked. As Mateo said, it looked like it was del año uno.

We lay there high as shit and traded questions about where we had grown up. I learned the internet had only come to this part of the island the year before, when they installed it at the school in the nearby village, but Mateo was immensely proud to tell me he had used it before then, at the library in Castro. I told him that yes, Las Vegas really was like the pictures, lit up neon against the sky, but because of all that you couldn't see the stars. I told him how much quieter it was in Chiloé, no cars, no hum of distant traffic or neighbors. That I had slept better the past three days than ever before. Something inside me withered, saying that out loud, but he didn't seem to be listening. He asked how old you had to be to play at the casinos. I leaned over and kissed him. I had never kissed anyone before, but I was a whole hemisphere away from anyone, any*thing* I knew, and that gave everything a dreamlike sheen. Mateo kissed me back, as a dream would.

A few minutes later, in the wardrobe, I think about taking his hand in my own to startle him into stopping his prayers, but instead leave it dangling limply at my side.

Dad slams the door behind him when he enters. It'll be him slamming the door, yes, because Mom will come in first, him trailing behind. Then she throws her purse down on the dusty floor in that exhausted manner she has, only to complain later about the scuffed leather.

"Philip?" Dad calls out to me, in an exhausted tone. "Hey, kid, we're back early."

The walls are paper thin, the bedroom door wide open. I hear it all. Even then, I start to visualize them—their postures, expressions, where they must stand. Dad at the stairwell, one foot on the bottom step, calling up in that hunched, sheepish posture I've seen my whole life. An old soccer injury makes it hard for him to climb stairs. "Philip!" he shouts again, more impatient. To my mother—"I don't think they're here."

"Of course they are." Her eyes roll. "We're in the middle of nowhere. Where would they go?"

Dad stays silent a minute, probably scratching at a stain on the wall or pulling at a sliver on the stairway banister. "You'd be surprised," he says finally. "Mateo lives here. He'll know the paths through these woods."

Mom steps past him up the stairs, saying my name half-heartedly a few times. At the top of the stairway her voice becomes more forceful. I imagine she stands up straighter, trying to summon whatever energy will be required if I'm not here. It's her nature to panic, and she'll presume me dead before Dad can even get a word in.

The floorboards by the doorway creak. There's a thin sliver of light that enters the wardrobe between its two doors, but I don't dare put my eye to it. Instead I pull back farther into the hanging clothes, wondering how clean they are. Beside me Mateo has ceased his prayers and seems to be holding his breath.

We should have just greeted my parents when they got back, I realize—to hell with whether we smelled like pot, whether they could tell we're high, how obvious it was we'd been slacking off all day instead of doing the chores they'd assigned. But after Mateo's nightmarish face at the sound of the door opening, the only thing I could think to do was hide, and now if they open the wardrobe and see us crammed together between these old clothes they'll know something significant is afoot.

"Goddamn it, Philip," my mother mutters on the other side of the wardrobe door. "You ass."

For a moment I think this means she somehow sees me. Then I understand she thinks she's alone. The resignation in her voice is something I've never heard before.

"Is he up there?" Dad calls from below. His footsteps start reluctantly up the stairs.

Mom walks across the room—I can't see her, of course, can't see anything, but I hear her feet on the floor, the floorboards creaking. As I grow older I will mull every moment over in my mind, filling in all the little details, everything that I could not see that day but can see so clearly now.

She sits cross-legged on the edge of the bed, shutting her eyes. She takes a deep breath. This is her centering technique. It means she's about to explode. Surely they were expecting me and Mateo to be here diligently working, so they could give Mateo a ride back to his place when we were done.

I hear Dad arrive in the doorway and he hovers there, waiting for her to open her eyes. He doesn't want to startle her. He's a skinny, hunched man even at forty, the scruff on his cheeks he doesn't shave often already gone gray. He looks at my mother lovingly, but wearied. His stomach's been unsettled since he got here, the combination of jet lag and the change of diet sending him to the bathroom often and for prolonged periods. This B and B is in much worse shape than Yaco let on in his letters. He has to know he won't see any return on his investment for years, if ever. Worse, he knows Mom knows it too.

Mom opens her eyes and lets them drift toward my father. "Your son isn't here," she says, and a smile plays at the corner of her lips. It's the cliché joke they both enjoy, that it's always *your son* when I do something wrong.

"*My* son?" he replies, probably with a raised eyebrow. "I haven't seen any paternity papers."

I've heard this all a million times. Then his voice grows softer, with a slight lilt upward, like you might speak to a child. It's hard not to read this tone as condescending. "You want to talk about what happened back there?"

The position of his voice tells me he doesn't join her on the bed but remains in the doorway, as if the ground between them is littered with mines.

She slips off her shoes and rubs the ball of her right foot. "Not really," she says, without looking up.

"I feel like we made a bit of a scene," he says.

"You should talk. Speaking about Philip that way in front of a pair of strangers."

My pulse quickens at the mention of my name. I keep my breath slow, shallow, quiet, caught between my two desires: for them to leave and to hear whatever happened. They teach English in the schools here but not well, so I'm not sure what if anything Mateo understands. I don't dare look at him because of the sound turning my head might make.

What did my dad say about me? I can only imagine. But I'll think back on this afternoon again and again in the years to come, and at times convince myself I have it all figured out with something approaching certainty.

A couple hours earlier, at the only restaurant in the village, my mother sat down at their tiny table apprehensively. She usually found Chilean food quite bland, and she had a bottle of Tabasco stashed in her purse to spice up whatever they put in front of her when Dad wasn't looking. It was something I'd insisted she pack for the trip, and up to then we'd both been glad she did.

But my father had always told us the food in Chiloé was better than that of the mainland, that they were both bland but chilote food was, "you know, *good* bland. Simple, pure, authentic." Mom was about to learn he was right. They sat outside, overlooking the ocean, smelling the breeze off the water. There was no menu—the server just rattled off the handful of dishes that could be prepared, all seafood freshly caught and lightly seasoned with butter, herbs, and lemon. Mom ordered salmon and could have died at how good it tasted. She drank white wine by the glass, while everyone else had local beer. She'd wondered aloud our first night in Chile, upon seeing a drink list, why anyone would order beer instead of some of the best, cheapest wine in the world.

It was still early for lunch, only twelve thirty. Thinking of my mother, Dad had requested they eat at that hour, knowing how accustomed she was to North American mealtimes. I'd heard him pitch it to Yaco and his wife as a "leisurely" meal the night before, and indeed it was. They sat a long time after they had all finished their food, telling tales of people the two men had known back when, my mother smirking at the idea that Dad really remembered all these people clearly from when he was six. She and Yaco's wife would interject the occasional question to clarify, *Now who was that?* or *Is that the man I met when... ?*, nothing of sincere interest. Though hers was excellent, Mom was tired of speaking Spanish by then, even with two weeks of the trip still ahead of her. The half-second pause it sometimes took her to decode the heavily accented Chilean slang or to organize her thoughts in her second language was often just enough for her to miss the chance to make a joke or divert the conversation to a topic she could relate to. During the trip, I'd caught her spacing out more and more as people talked around her. At lunch, she focused on the unseasonably springlike climate, the warm sun on her cheeks. She even shut her eyes a moment, basking in the sunshine, and listened as the conversation ambled toward us kids.

Children are given too much leeway these days, Yaco said. You never caught me stealing chicha when I was Mateo's age. His wife murmured her agreement.

Mom opened her eyes to see Dad tip the last bit of his beer into his mouth and motion at the server for another. It's the way it is now, he said. Children are the bosses. We might as well be chauffeurs.

Mom frowned. Dad didn't have a lot of male friends, and hearing the way he talked to Yaco, she was glad. Yaco was a large man: part mapuche with broad shoulders, dark skin, and arms as big as my father's thighs. Our first night there we saw him hold a chainsaw one-handed to chop a tree branch down for kindling. It must have irked him that Mateo was so slender and quiet-mannered, like his mother. Just as it probably irked my own father that neither he nor I knew how to help with that fire.

In our family, Dad was the pushover, plain and simple. Whenever I had earned some punishment, Mom had to be the one to dole it out, lest she risk me talking Dad out of it altogether. I had learned to go to him if I wanted something, anything from a GameCube to an ear piercing—both real examples, both cases where Mom intervened. Hearing him complain about whatever leniency they gave me had to have bothered her.

Yaco said, managing a tone that was both apologetic and accusatory, Usually, Mateo is not like this. He knows not to disobey.

Mom glanced at Dad, but he was now picking with great concentration at the label of the fresh bottle of beer the server had just brought. This was a habit he indulged in at home, too, and Mom was usually the one to throw these peeled-off labels away.

Yaco's gruffness toward Mateo was apparent to all of us the night before when they had found us together in Mateo's bedroom, leaning off each other on the bed, wet-lipped and passing the jarra between us. Yaco immediately began to bellow but Mom had insisted a day of chores was more than enough punishment. Now Yaco's tone was airing this grudge not so subtly. What would he have done, kept the kids apart for the rest of their trip? Something worse? She shuddered to think. She'd always made sure that any punishment was administered evenhandedly, free of anger. As a little boy I'd been overly sensitive, buried in books, quick to tears, and her perception of me had not yet grown beyond that.

Usually, Mom said, stressing the word with an uncharacteristic lack of nuance, we don't leave alcohol lying around where any pair of teenagers can get at it. This was true, as far as she knew. They had a lock on the liquor cabinet, though at the request of one of my friends I had made a copy of the key.

Dad reached for her hand where it lay clenched on the table. She drew it away, back to her lap. She shied away from public displays of affection, even under normal circumstances, but still he winced at this pulling away, wanting so badly to project contentment in front of this friend he hadn't seen in so long. Of course Yaco's tone would have bothered him too, but he was the type of man to ignore that, to just sip at his beer and let that flare of annoyance fade, then listen later in feigned surprise back at the B and B as Mom detailed just how badly the barb had stuck her.

Dad forced a dry laugh and said, against his better judgment, I'm sure if we did leave it out Philip would steal it, though.

The server brought a bajativo—a small glass of passion-fruit-flavored liqueur, on the house to help with digestion. While Dad was still thinking of a toast and about to raise his glass, Mom downed hers.

She said, Philip never stole a thing in his life, and has no idea what *chicha* is anyway. You think he saw that gross brown jar smelling of ferment and thought, *Oh, I want that?* Obviously, it was Mateo's idea.

Dad's fingers, which had resumed picking at the beer label, paused at their work. Before he could finish formulating a response, Yaco interjected jovially: Say what you will about my son, but spare my homemade chicha!

They all laughed. Even my mother smiled. It should have ended there. Then my father said, in that stubborn manner he had sometimes that came out of nowhere: No, you're right, Yaco. It's too much leeway we give them. You should see how picky Felipe is with his food. He still makes his mother peel his oranges, says the rind hurts his fingers. He won't kill a spider, he calls for one of us instead. He fusses with his hair for forty-five minutes every day before school. Can you imagine that, a kid unable to peel an orange? There were no kids like that when I was his age.

Yaco forced an anxious chuckle and shrugged. His wife laughed too, as if my father had just shared something as innocuous as a knock-knock joke. My father's hands lay limp in his lap, his shoulders slumped, his eyes not meeting my mother's gaze.

She crumpled her paper napkin and threw it on the table. Philip, she said. Our son's name is Philip, not Felipe. And I'd like to be taken back now, please.

"Look, I'm sorry I said all that," Dad says, still in the doorway. "About the oranges, about all the rest. All I meant was I wish you wouldn't worry over him so much. It's probably why he's afraid to put himself out there, you know? Why he won't play sports. Why he's so quiet around new people."

My face and neck burn with embarrassment. In the wardrobe I hope Mateo can't understand, isn't watching me, doesn't smell my sweat. I still can't see my parents, only guess at their movements.

"Quiet around new people," Mom repeats. "Like you with my friends."

"That's different. This isn't about me."

Mom lets out a short, huffy sort of laugh.

"Okay, fine," Dad says, still at the doorframe, probably clenching the jamb tighter now. "What if it is about me? I thought Philip might like it here. Might feel some connection. But he's more interested in getting in trouble with Mateo than he is in hearing about Chiloé, than seeing the island."

Mom's hands are likely on her knees now, as if steadying herself. "And what I was saying was that Mateo probably pressured him into that, into stealing the chicha. Same as he pressured him into ditching out on the chores here."

Dad frowns. "Well, then, he shouldn't let himself be bullied into things."

Mom is a tall, well-tanned woman, who at her full height towers over my father, but in anger her posture curls. There on the bed I'm sure she looks as if she might compress into a tight, irate ball he will never pry open. "Last time I checked," she says, "you're not such a tough old chilote yourself. I know more about building a campfire than you. I know how to gut a fish too. Maybe I'm chilota, what do you think?"

"That's not funny," Dad says. He stands up a little straighter, maybe puffs out his chest. "I can do those things, too."

Mom puts her face in her hands, not wanting to look at my father, maybe not wanting to look at any of her surroundings. I can tell by the muffled sound of her voice. "God, what century is this?" she says. "I was only joking. It doesn't matter if you can't gut a fish, just like it doesn't matter if your son would rather talk comics or whatever with Mateo instead of hang out with his fucking parents and a couple adults he doesn't know."

"Would it have killed him to take an interest in *something*?" Dad says.

She removes her hands from her face and glares at him. "Well, now he has! Congratulations. He is probably wandering around lost in the forest, communing with nature and island spirits and about to be bitten by some poisonous bug. Break open the champagne." She mimes opening a bottle, makes a popping sound with her lips. "The nearest neighbor is, what'd you say, three miles away? That's three miles of forest to be lost in!"

"It's kilometers, not miles, and anyway Mateo knows the forests. They won't be lost."

"How do you know?"

"Because I'm from here, too."

"Oh, come on."

"Come on, what?"

She shoots him a look that could peel paint. Dad once described to me how they met in philosophy class in college, how her anger at the other students who wanted to laugh off Descartes' thought experiments excited something in him. Now that anger turns toward him.

"I'm sorry," she says, "but I'm not sure your experience from fucking seventy-two is really relevant here. Anyway, I've seen Castro, the area where *you* grew up. You weren't exactly roughing it, you know?"

Dad says nothing in response. He takes a coin from his pocket and starts to roll it across his knuckles, an old habit from back when he quit smoking and needed something to do with his hands. Or no, he puts his index finger absently to his scalp, feeling beneath the hair for the scar where he clumsily ran into a branch playing tag when I was three. I've seen his hand drift there before.

Or perhaps he just stands there in the doorway, still and silent, like an animal holding its breath before a passing predator. Mom's eyes go to the grimy window in the corner of the room.

"You're right," he says finally. "I should have come here by myself. I don't know why I bothered bringing you. Either of you."

"That's not what I'm saying," Mom says quietly. She doesn't take her eyes off the window. Then, suddenly, like she just thought of it: "You know, I was born in Kalamazoo."

"Yes," he says impatiently, "I know."

She looks at him as if surprised by his response. "Do you?" Then, in a more assured, angrier tone: "Because I don't talk about it much. I have friends I've known for years who don't know that about me. We moved when I was three, for God's sake. You moved when you were what, five?"

"Six. And it's not the same."

"Six years old. A whole other part of the island. And here you are so confident that because you never got lost in the forests your son won't either. Your son who's barely ever been outside Nevada."

"I'm telling you, he's got Mateo."

"You don't know anything about Mateo! You think I'd try telling someone how to get from one end of Kalamazoo to the other? Or anything about what it means to be a child in Michigan in 2005?"

"It's not the same," he says again. There's an edge to it now, a raw quality. I can see him as that six-year-old chilote boy: uprooted, unmoored, clenching his fists and stomping his feet.

"Because I don't know the first goddamn thing about navigating Kalamazoo. I'd have to ask for help. Here, the nearest help is three kilometers away."

"It's not—"

"I know, I know, it's not the same. Why the hell not? What's different?"

"Because you could go back to Kalamazoo whenever you wanted!" he screams, and slams his fist into the wall.

Mateo and I both jump. It's a miracle neither of us bump the wardrobe door open. Now it's quiet out there, and I don't know why. I'm afraid they've heard the movement.

"God, Dalton, I didn't—"

"It's fine," he says quickly, in a barely human croak I've never heard before. He lets out a deep, shuddering sigh. He turns and leaves the room.

My mother sits on the bed, collecting herself. Downstairs, the front door creaks open then bangs shut. After a moment—perhaps just barely too long—she stands up and goes after him.

Chile was the last country in the Western hemisphere to legalize divorce, in 2004. Before that, marriage law was governed by a legal code written in the nineteenth century. But for a wealthy Chilean couple who could afford an annulment, the process was exceedingly easy. They had only to claim that a piece of information on the wedding certificate was wrong—their home address, for example. With that the whole marriage was not just terminated but nullified, as if it had never happened. I wonder if there are still Chileans who regret the loss of this ability to rewrite history. And I wonder if my parents would have been sure enough of their bond to marry if their culture and class had rendered that decision irreversible.

In 2007, when my father left us, I was convinced that whatever insurmountable barrier existed between him and my mother had to do with Chiloé: the fight they'd had, the outburst I'd heard from the wardrobe. After that trip, something shifted in him. He no longer asked for bottles of imported pisco for his birthday, and he didn't bother making chilote stew for the Chilean holidays. His arguments with my mother were less frequent, too. She eventually asked him if he could sleep in the second bedroom, since he snored, and he consented without a fuss.

But when he left us, it was not to return to Chiloé. He had met another woman, and moved to Florida to start a new life with her. They had a son soon after. I've only met him on Skype. I wonder if Dad talks with that son about Chiloé. I wonder if that son can peel an orange.

When we are sure we hear no movement in the house, Mateo and I emerge from the wardrobe. We walk quietly downstairs, to the front door, and peer out. Their rental car is parked on the lawn, but my parents are nowhere in sight. Beyond the car is the main road, completely abandoned, to the left a dense thicket of trees. It's where they must have gone. You can't see more than a few feet into it. I hope my dad's sense of direction is still what he says it is.

We should start hauling those boxes down, I say. Tuck that weed into your beltline. We'll say we took a break and went for a hike.

Of course, Mateo says. His expression is quizzical. He looks somehow even younger than before, positively childlike, or maybe I just feel that much older. But we did it! he says. We're safe now. He glances around excitedly, then moves to touch my cheek with his hand. I block it gently with my own. He looks startled. I am, too. An hour ago I was planning to spend any moment we had alone for the rest of the trip groping him. But seeing my parents like that, knives at each other's throats, and hearing what they had to say about me . . .

Their car's still here, I say again, voice as even as I can manage. They'll be back any minute.

By the time my parents return, most of the boxes have been hauled down. At a certain point we stopped bothering to really sort through them and decided anything left here this long had to be worthless. We're sitting on the porch, our backs against the house's old wood wall, legs stretched out before us, taking another break. Mom and Dad come out of the trees, him now a couple steps behind her. Mom raises her hand hello. I raise my hand back. Dad's eyes are on the ground, the car, the house, the road leading away—anywhere but meeting mine.

There, There

THE WIFE WANTED a cat, so they got a fish. They called him Bubbles, or Bubs for short. It was after a character in a TV show.

You go to work all day, the man told his wife. Who would take care of a cat?

The man was having trouble finding good work. He had a master's degree with a concentration in eighteenth-century German philosophy and taught intro courses at the local community college. He didn't work that much and when he did work it wasn't very hard. So they got a fish and he grew to love the fish. He got it an underwater castle to swim in and out of. Feeding it fish pellets was a welcome break from his day. Then the fish died, and he was angry with the wife.

He wanted to say a lot of things, but he didn't know how. What are we going to do with an empty fishbowl? he asked her.

She was standing outside the bathroom. The empty bowl was in her hands, the toilet still running. We should get a dog, she said. Its life span is longer.

Absolutely not, the man said. Dogs are expensive and they slobber all over everything. Plus we don't have a yard. Dogs need a yard.

They settled on a box turtle and an aquarium to put it in. The man bought a large water bowl and took the castle from the fishbowl and put these in for decoration. The wife didn't tell him how out of place the castle looked, and he was happy for that. They called the turtle Raphael.

Every day the man walked to the pet store down the street and bought a bag of live crickets. He tossed them one at a time into the aquarium and watched the turtle go on the hunt. When it caught one it extended its neck out of its shell and its beak-like mouth cut the crickets in half. The man would smile at that and dump another one in.

Then one day the man woke up and there was a small bump on the turtle's neck. The next day it swelled bigger. The day after that it was the size of a small grape. They took it to the vet and it didn't make it back home with them. The husband was distraught. Now it's a whole aquarium! he said, fighting back tears. It seemed such a waste. A glass aquarium in the corner of the room, empty except for the water bowl and toy castle. An emptiness that stared back at him stubbornly, after all the trouble he went to making such a comfy home for Raphael.

There, there, the wife said.

What she really wanted was a baby, but she knew better than to ask for that just yet. So instead they got a cat, and named it Kyle MacLachlan. This the husband did not like.

The cat was friendly with the wife, but all day while she was at work it just lazed around. It would nap on the sofa, then the bed, then the kitchen table. If the husband wanted to sit down somewhere, that's where the cat would be napping. He tried to give it treats, and the damn thing just stared at him. He tried to pet it, and it hid under the bed. The man frowned. What was the point of a cat, anyway?

Then there was the meowing. Incessant, that was the word for it.

When it wasn't sleeping the cat would trail him around the house, glaring up at him, letting out short, sharp meows like the barks of a dog. He tried to read. Meow! He tried to grade papers. Meow! He tried giving it more food, more water, more toys, more anything it could want. Meow! it still said. Meow meow!

What!? the man finally yelled one day. What do you want from me!?

The cat rubbed itself against his leg and meowed insistently. Then it hopped up onto the back of the sofa and stared out the window, still meowing. The man thought he understood. For a moment he felt very sad. There was a whole world out there the cat could see but never touch, never smell. Cars zoomed by on the street, planes flew noisily overhead, the sun painted the sky new colors each day. Leaves grew green on the trees then withered and fell away. A whole world spun by outside without them.

But he couldn't let the cat go outside. You can't train a cat, not well. They won't wear a leash. And out there, beyond the window, beyond the home they had made, there were all sorts of dangerous things. Coyotes, disease, hapless drivers. So many neck growths and empty aquariums.

Please, just be here with me, the man whispered to the cat. Let me be enough for you. He put his hand to the back of its neck. For once, the cat let him pet him.

The Brightmore Problem

JIM McFIDDLE, THE mailman, was the first to voice concern. It was six o'clock on a Saturday evening, and like usual he was in Jen's Tavern, the only bar in Brightmore. He had his blue mailbag sitting next to him, filled with letters he hadn't had time to deliver that day. So far Jim had drunk three beers. He ordered a fourth and while Jen the barkeep refilled his glass he sprinkled salt on his coaster. He didn't like it to stick to the bottom of the glass.

"Lately I feel like my days go by faster and faster," he said to Jen. He took a big gulp of beer. Out loud it sounded like a small admission, but he felt a great load lift as he said it, a heaviness he hadn't even noticed before. His days had indeed been slipping by at far greater speed than ever before. He was able to deliver less and less mail each day before dark, and each morning he felt like he'd barely had time to shut his eyes before the clock started to buzz. At night when he came home and made love to his wife, he could only make her come once before they had to get to sleep, if even that. But it didn't seem like he was doing any of these things slower or less efficiently than usual. He would just glance up at the clock and suddenly realize what had felt like a half hour was a full hour, what had felt like only a decent start was by now surely making his wife sore.

Of course, he didn't say all this to Jen. He just said his days were going faster. To his shock her eyes got real wide. She took the bar rag off her shoulder and started wringing it excitedly in her hands. "You know, I feel the same way?" Jen said. "Like all of a sudden time is evaporating on me."

There were murmurs of assent along the bar. Sam Kingsley, sitting beside Jim, said he was able to fix fewer television sets every day. Eleanor Bunker said she practically had to sprint from gas meter to gas meter to get the right readings. Todd Moss, the kindergarten teacher, told them all reluctantly he was teaching their children a little less each day. Last year by this time the young crop could all spell simple words; this year they barely knew their ABCs.

Jim's mouth hung open a little. He looked from bar patron to bar patron. He hadn't meant to stir up anything, and frankly if it wasn't for all their faces looking so sincerely astonished he would have thought they were pulling his leg. "Well, it's just a feeling I got is all," Jim said. "I'm sure it's nothing." He was a practical man. If nothing could be done about a thing, he thought it best not to pay that thing any mind. He shouldn't have opened his mouth in the first place.

Jen looked from Jim to the other customers. She started to fan herself with a drink menu. "Nuh-uh," she said. "That's no good for me. I'm positively freaked out." She poured herself a shot of whiskey with a Coke back, though normally she waited until at least eight before she started drinking at work.

Sally Huntsberger, the woman who ran Brightmore Shop and Pawn, had hitherto been quiet. She, like Jim, was a practical person, but she felt like she ought to speak up, even if it made her look the fool. "I don't know how to tell you all this," she said, "but it gets worse."

She pulled an old clock out of her purse and set it on the bar. She knew her eyes were shot through with red lines, and she hoped she didn't look too crazy. What little sleep she'd gotten lately counted for less and less. She'd taken to carrying this analog clock, a small black boxy thing someone had pawned, around with her and taking it out whenever she had a moment alone. She figured she was the first to make the discovery. Nobody carried watches anymore, they just used their phones.

She asked Jen to turn down the radio. Jen did. Sally let the clock sit there and said she didn't notice anything at first. And then when she did, she thought the problem was just this particular clock. "But it's not the clock," Sally said. "It's every clock, every watch. It's happening everywhere. Listen."

The bar became very still as they all listened. It let out a rough, metallic click with each second. It seemed strange that anyone would want a clock so loud, Jim thought. It was bound to drive one crazy after a while.

"My god," Jen said.

Todd Moss popped his knuckles nervously.

"What?" Jim asked. "I don't hear anything."

"At first I thought it was just this clock," Sally repeated. "But it's every clock. They're all like this." She started to count along with the beat of the second hand. "One missus, two missus, three missus, four . . ."

"It's so fast," Jen said.

Sally nodded. "And it's getting worse. It was so slight at first I thought it was my imagination. I could get through a solid 'one mississip' before we were on to the next second." She pulled out her phone and went to time.gov for the official US time. "Look," she said. "It's the same. One missus, two missus, three missus . . ."

They were all spooked by the revelation. Even Jim, who was still trying to convince himself that there was some reasonable explanation, that they were making a big deal out of what had been only an innocent comment. Someone turned on the news and they watched the clock at the bottom. It lined up perfectly with what Sally's phone said, and very nearly with what the pawned clock said. After that there seemed a general consensus that all that could be done was to tie one on. There were a couple rounds of top-shelf whiskey on the house. They all speculated forlornly what "aged ten years" could really mean to anyone now.

"It means we've all got less time left than ever before," Todd said sadly. Jim replied that that had always been true for everybody anyway, at each given moment, and finished his whiskey in one great gulp.

When Jim got home that night, he was so drunk he could barely stand. He finally slumped into bed at two in the morning, and his wife, Hannah, was already asleep. She'd declined his invitation to join him at the tavern, said she was tired and had a headache. He started to press himself up against her clumsily and kissed her ear and the side of her neck. She woke up just enough to elbow him away. "In the morning," she said. "I'm trying to sleep."

He lay there a long while staring at the digital clock on his nightstand as his wife snored beside him. He watched the minutes fall away. He told himself it was all some trick of the clock in the bar. Or a bad cell phone connection, bad TV reception. Something was off in the technology somewhere, that was all. And even if there really was something off with the time (which there wasn't), it's not like anyone could do anything about it anyway. He tried to count to sixty Mississippi to see if it lined up with a minute on his bedside clock but he kept losing count. He knew if he and Hannah could just get it on, he could have her quivering with pleasure in no time, faster than ever. That would prove Sally wrong, he thought to himself. He shut his eyes and went to sleep.

The next day Jim woke with a hangover that felt like holy judgment on all his misdeeds. His head hurt something terrible, and his guts were knotted up inside his stomach. He spent his morning on the toilet, doing all he could not to doze off. Thankfully it was Sunday, so there was no mail to deliver. He felt as if he'd gotten almost no sleep at all.

That afternoon, when he was finally feeling right in the head again and had chalked up the revelations of the night before to alcohol-inspired paranoia, he got a call from Sally Huntsberger.

He was lying on his couch watching reruns of *Cheers* when his phone started to buzz. It wriggled its way toward him on the coffee table. He didn't recognize the number but the area code was Brightmore so he picked it up and said hello.

"Jim," she said. "It's Sally Huntsberger."

Jim sat up on the couch and looked around. His house was rather large, and it seemed Hannah was at the other end of it. He thought he remembered her saying something about going to lie down awhile. That was good. He wanted to put the nonsense of the night before behind him, and if he could avoid having to explain it to his wife then that was all the better.

"What do you want, Sally?" he said quietly into the phone. It came out harsher than he'd meant it.

On the other end, Sally laughed. "It's good to talk to you, too," she said. Then she explained excitedly that she'd woken up that morning with, as she put it, "a wild hair up her ass" and decided to do a little bit of digging on what she kept calling the "Brightmore Problem."

He wanted to interrupt her, to tell her there was no reason to let their drunken musings from the night before get them all bent out of shape, but there didn't seem to be a suitable pause in her ravings. And besides, he wanted to be careful not to say anything too specific his wife might hear. Sally explained that there seemed to be no temporal deviation from the night before as of yet, things were holding steady around "one missus," both on the pawnshop clock (exhibit A) and on time.gov (exhibit B). Then she'd found what she called a "control group" (here Jim was fairly sure she was not using this term correctly) in little Billy Baptist, who was riding his bike on the street. She'd had him count along with the pawnshop clock and he'd also gotten through "n missus" with each tick of the second hand. This showed the problem was not isolated to "us older folks." Like Jim, Sally was in her early forties.

But this is when things got real strange, Sally said. Because this all had her so freaked out she'd decided to go see her sister Sam, who lived on a farm outside Yawpton, maybe fifty miles away. She'd arrived nearly incoherent, bursting into tears as she drove up the long dirt drive to the farmhouse. Her sister's husband was sure it was something some man had done, and kindly offered to kick the crap out of whoever that was. And when she'd gotten inside, blubbering incoherently and unable to speak, she'd pulled the clock out of her purse and tried to demonstrate her findings to her sister and her sister's husband. And then, to both her horror and also her great relief, the clock ticked off the seconds at a reasonable speed, there in her sister's house: one Mississippi, two Mississippi, three Mississippi, four.

Now Sally hadn't known what to think. She'd accepted some tea from her sister and said it was nothing, the problem was nothing, just man troubles she'd rather not talk about, she just needed to get away for an afternoon. On her way back to Brightmore, though, Sally had set the pawnshop clock on the seat beside her. Every so often, she'd count along. Sure enough, the seconds got quicker as she neared Brightmore. Twenty miles out it was n mississip. Ten miles out n mississi. Then, as you crossed the town limits, it was back down to n missus.

"It's Brightmore," Sally whispered into the phone, her voice betraying fear and wonder. "The problem is Brightmore."

Jim glanced down the hall at the cracked door of the bedroom. He rubbed at a knot in his lower back, a place grown stiff from all his time spent sitting down that day. He was so used to walking around delivering mail that he didn't do well with sitting anymore.

"Sally," he said, "do you think maybe you're still a little messed up from last night? That was some epic drinking there. I've been laid up all day."

"What are you talking about? Go to your computer yourself, watch the time tick. This is serious."

"What's that, honey?" Jim said to the empty room, only half covering his phone's mic. "Oh, okay. Listen, Sally, I'm afraid I'm going to have to let you go. The wife's calling."

With that he hung up the phone, leaving Sally mid-protest.

• • •

Sally was in her shop, watching a couple customers poke around, making sure they didn't steal anything. "It's not like this is just you and me," she said to the empty line, not realizing Jim had hung up. "Todd, Jen, Eleanor, Sam. They all heard it too. It's our lives being stolen here. Second by second. Seconds add to minutes. And besides," she said, cupping her hand so she could whisper right into her phone, "this could be huge. This throws a wrench in the whole works. It revises our whole conception of space and time and all that."

Her attention was drawn back to her customers. Aside from pawned goods, the shop sold a small selection of snacks and groceries. Her customers, a young couple who lived down the street, were trying to decide between a full gallon or half gallon of milk. They tried to do the math to figure out the price difference. "How many pints in a quart?" she heard one say. "So this is, like, eight beers' worth?"

On the other end of the phone, there was silence. Sally looked down at the screen and saw the call had ended. She put the phone down on the counter and stared at the boxy black clock beside it. She wondered what was the last thing Jim had heard. She waited impatiently while the young couple abandoned the milk plan and bought a carton of cigarettes instead and, when no one came in after they left, she wrote *Gone for a beer* on a loose leaf of notebook paper and taped it to the outside of the shop door.

Sally walked across the street to the tavern. Jen was behind the bar again, and Eleanor was there too, eating a hamburger. "You folks remember what we talked about last night?" Sally asked them. "The clocks and whatnot?"

Eleanor shifted in her seat uncomfortably. Jen ran a rag over a glass and held it up to the light with one eye closed. Sally watched them share a glance. "We were mighty tipsy last night," Eleanor said simply.

Sally took out her phone and showed her time.gov. Eleanor shrugged. "If that's what they say it is, that's what it is," she said.

Sally would have no better luck later that day, when she visited Todd at the school during afternoon naptime. "Must just be us getting older," he said, shrugging when he had to wake the children up off their baby blue blankets after what seemed like no time at all. She tried to tell him what had happened at her sister's house, but he interrupted her to say he didn't have time for this. They both winced at his choice of words.

Part of Sally was unsurprised at this lack of interest for what she had to say. The thing people liked about Brightmore was precisely how unremarkable it was. The same shops opened and closed at the same time each day, the same people crowded Jen's Tavern Friday nights for the fish fry, the same roads led to the same nowhere places. People left, sure, especially the young ones, but it was rare that they did not return sooner rather than later. There was a sense among Brightmore folk that you could go anywhere in America (save the big cities) and find the same sort of people, the same flavors of fried fish, the same sun-faded brick. In this way life in Brightmore was a comforting lull. Time seemed to stand still, though the clocks told Sally how fast it was galloping forward.

Back at the Shop and Pawn later that evening, Sally logged on to what she thought of as "the office computer." She didn't have one at home, but she spent most of her time here anyway. The store had started off as something just for groceries, like a convenience store but a little cheaper than the Gas N' Dash on the corner up the road. But over time Sally had realized that so many people in Brightmore had things they wanted to discard. Things they wanted a home for. Clothes their children had outgrown, old guns and spark plugs, old textbooks they had no problem selling though they were property of Brightmore Public, jewelry they inherited but had no occasion to wear.

Now Sally opened up a browser and, typing with her two-finger method like a hen pecking seed, pointed it to Google.

Sally had no head for research, but she did her best to scour Wikipedia articles for possible explanations of the problem in Brightmore. She read until her eyes ached, and even considered donning the pair of bifocals someone had exchanged for a new stapler to see if that helped. Instead she went to the liquor shelf and popped the cap off a bottle of

Kessler. She filled the cap and sipped at the thimble-sized shot, deep in thought.

From what she could tell, there was little chance of the US government's clock having been corrupted, though the definition of a second was a thing she couldn't quite grasp yet. Something to do with the speed of a certain particle behaving a certain way. The government had big fancy machines that measured this behavior. Besides, she'd cross-checked with the Greenwich Mean Time, and the Brits' clock gave her the same problem. What's more, the problem was Brightmore, only in Brightmore; that meant it couldn't be the measurement apparatus in some remote place, it had to be something there in her hometown, right before her unbespectacled eyes.

Most modern clocks ran on electricity somehow, either a phone picking up radio signals or the electrified materials in a clock vibrating at a certain regular frequency. Could it be that electricity itself somehow behaved differently in Brightmore? But then, this was the twenty-first century. Time was relative—they'd known that for almost a hundred years. Perhaps space-time was curved some certain weird way, bunching around Brightmore like a frumpy dress might pile up around your middle. But then, why wouldn't the clocks themselves be caught up in that space-time frumpiness, why wouldn't they have the same time sense as Sally and the rest of them?

Then there was the final possibility, the one Sally didn't much care for. That somewhere along the way she'd gone bonkers, and this was the world's way of letting her know. That through some strange vibrations she was giving off she'd caused a sort of localized mass hysteria the night before at the pub, and through the power of suggestion and the haze of alcohol gotten the others to go along with her in her madness.

No, Sally thought. It was Jim, not her, who brought it up. And besides, listen to the clock there now. One missus, two missus. She counted along with it, the tick a gentle assurance of her sanity, a gentle assurance that it was the world, not her, that was unintelligible.

• • •

In high school, the blue Science Fair ribbon had always been Sally's for the taking. And not just because there were only a few others who entered each year; science and math, those were her things. She was sure these skills would have served her well if she had bothered to go on to college. Though she never had children—never had much luck with men either, having been told she was too "opinionated"—she had toyed with the idea of adoption, because damn if it wouldn't be a treat to help a kid with a Science Fair project.

Now Sally unearthed this long-buried interest. People who came into the store from that point on consistently saw her slouched over her keyboard at the counter, pecking away. Occasionally someone would ask what she was working on. She'd glance at them, startled, and blink rapidly a few times like she needed to refocus her eyes to see something that wasn't words. She'd learned her lesson, though. People didn't want to hear what she had to say, and she didn't want to be labeled "eccentric." (Though despite her caution, she was well on her way to earning this label.) Her fake answers would vary widely and included "fan fiction," "a romance novel," "letters to the editor," "slam poetry," and "the great American novel."

Here's where her interlocutor would nod slightly, hands in pockets, not meeting her eye, and say something noncommittal, something like, "That sure is something, Sal." Sally would nod absently, eyes already back on the screen. Every so often, she would pick up the phone to call Jim. He seemed like the one person who might listen to her, the one person who was at least observant enough to have voiced his sense of things. She would give him updates, like that the speed seemed to have settled at n missus, showed no further signs of speeding up. But he would always just say that whatever the clocks said the clocks said, and there was no use paying it any mind. So eventually Sally stopped calling.

It wasn't long before the speakers at scientific conferences started trading snickers and pointed comments over a paper almost all of them had received. Invariably it had made it out of the slush pile and into the hands of an editor, not for quality but for sheer gall and unintentional humor. Entitled "The Brightmore Problem" and riddled with errors of spelling, grammar, and logic, the paper was clearly a (poorly perpetrated) hoax. It described a town in the middle of nowhere no one had ever even heard of, and how "space-time itself" seemed to behave strangely there. On the best days one of these presenters would have a copy of the paper with them, and they'd all take turns reading lines aloud and laughing hysterically.

When after several months Sally hadn't heard even a peep from the journals she had written to, she tried writing letters to newspaper and magazine editors. She drove diligently into the city every week to find the largest newsstand she could and flipped through the pages of all these publications to no avail. Her letters never appeared. So under the judgmental eyes of the newsstand owner she would buy herself a candy bar and make the long, silent drive home alone.

A year to the day after having that fateful conversation with Jim McFiddle and the other regulars at Jen's Tavern, Sally closed the shop early and hid herself inside to upload all her evidence to the internet. This was a thing she had been putting off for some time. Sooner or later someone from Brightmore would find these things, she knew, and she did not look forward to that day. Her experience discussing the problem with Jim and Eleanor and Tom and the rest had soured her on anyone from Brightmore ever taking her or her observations seriously. People in Brightmore just wanted to pass their days in obscure relaxation. It pained them too much to think there was something strange about the only town they'd ever known. That by remaining in the town they loved they were actively choosing to lead truncated lives.

Included in the evidence she uploaded was her paper, "The Brightmore Problem," along with videos she'd taken with various clocks, cell phones, and official times. She was always onscreen counting along, one missus two missus. She'd long ago noticed that cameras weren't subject to Brightmore time; the videos she uploaded would have counters at the bottom that said little more than thirty seconds, but there would be Sally on the screen, counting up to a full sixty missus along with time.gov. She uploaded all these things. Then, while she waited for the comments and emails to start coming in, she walked out to the front of the shop and taped up the *For Sale* sign she'd had prepared for some time.

When the shop sold to Kelly Biggleton, owner of the Gas N' Dash, Sally moved to the nearest big city and bought a new shop. There she sold general goods and pawned items at a much higher markup than before. She found she liked the big city, the bars she could go to wrapped in a comfortable layer of anonymity. She could get drunk every night of the week and never visit the same bar twice. She found a man in one of these bars and pretty soon she moved in with him and they lived together for many years. He didn't laugh when she told him about the Brightmore Problem, though he didn't seem all that concerned either, and she was afraid if she pressed it he'd think she was crazy.

Every once in a while someone would come into her shop to talk to her about Brightmore. She knew from the number of hits on her YouTube page and blog that many people had seen what she posted. Many of these comments were mean-spirited. Others applauded her effects work in making the clocks appear off, and wondered how she accomplished this. Some called it "interactive fiction," an attempt at bringing a little sci-fi color into the real world. She should start a Kickstarter, they told her. Surely her goal was to make a movie, right? And then there were the types who visited her shop sometimes, mostly younger people, people she called the True Believers. These people took her posts for what they were: real-life, unedited documents of a phenomenon she was unable to explain. They'd tracked her down based on her YouTube username, so similar to her real one. These people praised Sally for her courage. Sometimes they had visited Brightmore themselves. Often these conversations took an unfortunate turn when the visitors began to speak in lowered tones about government conspiracies and illuminati and evil lizard people waging secret wars.

Nevertheless, Sally was happy. She'd more or less given up on getting anyone other than a select few to believe her. She'd tried everything she could think of, and learned to content herself with that. The years rolled on at a comfortable pace—still a bit faster than she might have preferred, perhaps, but comfortable nonetheless. The man she was living with moved out and another moved in, and with that new man she had a wedding, though by that point they were both in their late fifties. She never sent her paper anywhere else. The number of hits on her web page stalled, and her YouTube subscribers started to fall. Sally didn't think about these things much. She forgot the password for the email associated with her YouTube and blog accounts, so she stopped getting any messages regarding them. Occasionally a True Believer would wander into her store, maybe someone who said they'd been to Brightmore, observed the phenomenon. Sally would shrug and smile politely. Invariably these people left her store acting as if they'd somehow been cheated, like Sally's lack of enthusiasm had dampened their own.

When Sally's brother-in-law died, she drove out to her sister's farm with her husband. The wake was at the farm. Sally was well aware of some strange looks she got as she walked in and she smiled to think about all the time she'd spent trying to avoid the label "eccentric." Most of these people had family in Brightmore, family who were aware of and none too happy with those mean, slanderous things Sally had posted what seemed like only yesterday. Sally shook everyone's hand and gave her sister her condolences. Then, after all the hangers-on had left, Sally started to feel an old tingle in her knees and fingers, an itchiness to satisfy a long-forgotten curiosity. So she discreetly told her husband to stay there with her sister, she was going to make a quick trip into Brightmore.

Jim was sitting on his living room couch with a beer in his hand when the doorbell rang. He called to his wife to see if she would get the door, but there was no answer. She was probably lying down. It was a Saturday afternoon and Jim had his feet propped up on a red and white cooler full of beer. His legs ached all the time now. He didn't want to stand up. He called to whoever was at the door to come on in already, it should be unlocked.

A woman roughly his age, early sixties, walked in tentatively. "Jim?" she asked. "That you?"

He eyed the woman and took a long, suspicious drink of beer. He said yes, it was him, and how could he help her.

"It's me, Sally," she said. "Sally Huntsberger."

Jim squinted. The woman's hair was streaked with gray, her skin mottled and bunched up in weird ways around her face. But it was Sally all right. The years had been rough on her but not so rough as on some. "So it is," Jim said. "Haven't been round in a while, eh?" He shifted uncomfortably in his seat, hoping his wife wouldn't mind him talking with this woman alone. He moved his feet and started to root around in the cooler.

"Beer," he said, and handed her one. He'd meant it like a question but it had come out a statement. Sally smiled and popped the tab and said thanks. She sat down.

"You been busy," Jim said. "I saw your videos."

Sally felt an excited tremor in her fingers as she brought the beer to her lips. She nodded. It felt strange to talk about this thing again after so long, though that was precisely why she'd come to see Jim. "I wanted to thank you," she said. "I don't know if you remember. It was something you said. We were in Jen's Tavern—is that still around? It was something you said that got me thinking maybe I wasn't just crazy."

Jim smiled toothily. Sally winced to see he'd lost a couple and hadn't bothered with fakes.

"It's 'cause of you I ended up leaving Brightmore," she said. "I just wanted to say thanks is all. I've got a husband now. Not that I don't respect your decision to stay."

"A husband," Jim said. "How about that." He took another drink. He was about six beers deep on his buzz and he was starting to feel light-headed, like it was hard to keep up with what this woman was saying. "I saw your videos," he said again. "On the internet, a long time ago."

Sally smiled and gazed down at the rim of her beer can, determined not to look too long at the gaps between Jim's teeth.

"How'd you do that?" Jim asked. "With the clock, I mean. How'd you make it run so fast?"

Something plummeted inside Sally. She'd been imagining this moment for some time, and it had always played out with some knowing comment of validation from Jim, something that showed there was at least one person in Brightmore who thought she was sane. She looked across the room at him. The beer in his hand, the puffy wrinkled skin around his eyes, the tinge of pink round his pupils. The red and white cooler and his crossed ankles on top of it, showing off the holes in his faded black socks. She strained to see the man she'd known so long ago, buried beneath the missing teeth and the wrinkles and all the years in a different stream of time.

She shook her head. She stood up, set her half-drunk beer on the coffee table, and clapped him on the shoulder. "Maybe I'll tell you sometime," she said. "Anyway, thanks for the beer."

For a long while after Sally left, Jim sat watching TV. He called to his wife but she was who knew where and didn't answer. He wanted to tell her Sally had stopped by. She was something of a Brightmore celebrity now, though perhaps more infamous than famous. He hadn't followed all that about him having said something long ago. He had trouble anymore following people who weren't Brightmore people. Like these folks on the TV, Norm and Cliff and all them *Cheers* folk. He used to love this show, but now it was so damn fast-paced. People zoomed in and out of the shots, babbling so rapidly, you could barely catch the jokes. The images flitting by on the screen started to lose all meaning, just a pleasant stream of shuffling photos too fast to assign a story to. He drank his beer and narrowed his eyes and concentrated so hard on the images and the lips and the garbled words that he started to get a headache and finally had to turn the damn thing off. He went to the window and looked out onto the street, wishing he'd known Sally better, Sally and her strange celebrity. Part of getting older, he guessed, to feel the world was passing you by. There at the window he finished his beer and watched the occasional car pass, the occasional child at play, as overhead the clouds galloped across the sky and the sun made its hasty descent toward the horizon.

Nothing Is Ever So Simple as Zombies

I KNOW YOU LOVE the things now, the way they are on TV. But they won't be so popular if they come for real.

They won't be evil, simply misguided. Not bloodthirsty, just wanting of a little human company. You will wake up and there's your mother at the door, your mother who's been dead ten years or more. Maybe even me, looking lost. You will know that me and Marie are dead, but won't want to be rude, so you'll have no choice but to open the door. You'll sit us down at the table with your family. You'll be eating rehydrated bread or nutrient pills or whatever the hell people eat by then. You'll say to your kids, "You remember Grandpa Tom. You remember Nana Marie."

We won't say anything in return, because our vocal cords will be long since decayed. You'll wonder, What did we ever say to each other anyway? Were their eyes this lifeless before, or is that new? What about the smell, the sunken gums? You'll have a hard time sitting there, trying to sort out the parents you remember from the ones who are there now. This will be anything but simple.

Your mother will make a whirring sound in the back of her throat like a malfunctioning garbage disposal, and your kids will try to imitate this sound. Your wife will hiss under her breath for them to stop, not to be rude. Soon, your children will be sauntering all around the house making this noise, "speaking zombie." This will annoy you to no end. You'll sit them down and try to impress upon them that it's not polite to make fun. When they say they're not, they're just trying to be closer to Grandma, you'll say, Some things are best left distant.

Though I always pictured a house in the country for you, big and affordable with a creek out back and maybe a chicken coop, you'll probably live in the city, or at best a house in the burbs that looks like all the other houses. I'll make that sound like a broken garbage disposal at you and I will mean, You should have lived out in the country. In the country you could put up chicken wire to make sure your mom and me don't wander off and scare the neighborhood.

You'll have no choice but to shut us up in the attic with all the boxes of crap you didn't get around to sorting through after we died. You'll tell your children, Don't worry, they like it up there. There are other parents in other attic windows, and they can wave to them, and they will wave back.

But we will be zombies, after all. You'll start to notice things after a while, things that make sleep difficult. Pained moans in the night, strange shufflings at all hours, the sound of fingernails scraping against the front door, like someone's trying to get out. You'll tell your children, Make sure you lock your door at night. Then there are the things we will leave behind, starting small: a blue tip of finger here, a pile of yellow teeth there. Finally a dark, withered ear found in the cookie jar, like the person who lost it felt ashamed and tried to hide it. You'll put a lock on the attic door and your wife will get mad. She'll say, This is a natural part of life. How will you feel if, when we're old and zombied, our children lock us up in the attic?

And when you wake up in the middle of the night and there I am, gnawing on some exposed part of your arm, you'll smack me with a folded magazine and tell me to shoo. It's just a phase, you'll say to yourself as I lumber out of the room, like a child teething. How long can parents stay zombies? And anyway, how much damage can they really do? He barely drew blood. You'll try not to think of those movies you watched when you were young, where if you were bitten that meant you were soon to turn.

The next night you'll show your children how to barricade the bedroom door, just in case. Just like in the movies, the ones where zombies attack—some two-by-fours from the construction yard, scrap metal from the garage, various riffraff from around the room. It will be fun, this parent-child bonding, in a bittersweet way. But this memory will loom in their minds, not as a memory about their grandparents but about their father, you, and how you handled me. It will be a lesson in the protections needed against family, and how to build walls when the time comes.

Sayings

AFTER AN ESPECIALLY petty argument with my wife, I became obsessed with the power of cliché. We had been arguing a lot lately, about a long list of hypotheticals in regard to the protuberance that was just starting to tent the shirt beneath her breasts: what would be the protuberance's name, would it attend private school or public, would it be circumcised or un-, would we make it take piano lessons like my parents made me, etc.

But the particular argument in which inspiration hit was over what to watch on television. I was in favor of *Tiny House Hunters*, thinking mistakenly the title referred to the size of the hunters not the houses, and she was for *So You Want to Be a Princess.* Neither of us felt strongly, but by that point argument had become our default mode of interaction.

I had been taking Xanax for anxiety, half a pill three times daily, and in the evenings I'd chase it with a splash of red wine drunk from a coffee mug. It left me with a pleasant, hazy feeling, and through this haze I had started to think perhaps there was more to the world than what I saw: Perhaps the laws of the universe weren't so steadfast as they seemed, and the people who got ahead did so because they knew how to ask the universe for whatever it was they wanted.

And in argument with my wife it occurred to me that maybe the way of asking could be found in cliché, that these oft-repeated phrases weren't like some scratched-up kitchen cutlery, dulled with age, but like a cast-iron skillet that gains flavor each time it's used. That the ritual chant of these phrases over decades or centuries might have imbued them with magic.

So I ceased shouting at my wife and instead stood up and spoke calmly, firmly: "We are watching *Tiny House Hunters*. That is final." As I said this I stamped my foot down on the floor as hard as I could. I even ground it into the carpet for good measure.

"What are you doing?" she asked.

"I'm putting my foot down."

She started to laugh, so I stomped my foot down again, even harder. The jolt of it pained my knee and lower back.

Her laugh and smile faded. She looked down at my foot and frowned. Finally she said, "Look, whatever, watch what you want."

I sat down beside her on the couch and took the remote in hand.

The next day I went to a gun store and bought a bullet. I told the camouflaged man behind the counter I wanted only one, but he made me buy the whole box. So I bought the whole box and buried all but one in the backyard.

From then on every time I had to do something unpleasant I would take the bullet discreetly from my pocket and slip it into my mouth. For instance, coming home from work, standing outside our apartment door, readying myself to insert my key. I would slip the bullet into my mouth and bite down thoughtfully. Thus having bit the bullet, I figured, I was ready to accept whatever lay on the other side of that door. And when it opened and there was my wife with a pamphlet in hand, ready to recite what she'd found about the best breathing exercises, or formula versus milk, or a book I should read to her belly at night, or some new pain in her body that needed to be rubbed, I found these things easier to accept. The lingering taste of metal filled me with a short euphoria, a tiny high, that dampened the immediacy of these household matters.

At work I kept the bullet in almost all day. My job was telephone customer service, and the customers thought I had some slight speech impediment. No one noticed my mouth bullet. When after a while the bullet's effect decreased, I unburied the box and extracted one more round. From then on I had two bullets to bite down on, sometimes simultaneously, whenever needed. I became an expert at rolling these slowly around my mouth with no one noticing, gently wedging them between my teeth. I was careful to keep them from the back of my throat, after once I ran to the bathroom gagging in the middle of an argument with my wife, having nearly swallowed them.

The time bomb in her stomach continued to tick. I love my wife. But that swelled gut jutting out at me began to seem like some line of an argument she was trying. How could I defend myself, any idea of mine, when she held in her belly the only thing nearly certain to outlast us both?

One night she rebuffed my advances, saying she didn't like the way she looked anymore, and swatted me away like some insistent fly. I knew that this would be the way it was for the rest of the pregnancy, another four months with no physical affection, and I excused myself from the room to go stand in front of the kitchen sink as one by one I cracked and emptied the contents of an eighteen-pack of eggs into the whirring garbage disposal, bullets in mouth, trying to concentrate on the proverbial omelet.

I let a million little rituals fill my life. To ease my anxiety at home, I ordered a heart-shaped box filled with expired Valentine's Day candy. I tried to eat a piece, a small square thing filled with nougat, but the chocolate had turned tough and bitter. So I threw away the candy and kept the box in my nightstand. I would feel right at home, I reasoned, because home is where the heart is. When it worked for only a matter of days I went to the butcher shop in the center of town and bought myself a beef heart, which I kept in the bottom drawer of the fridge where my wife never looked. I replaced it with a new one every week and as I did I felt a swell of welcome fill the house.

At work I started drinking Kool-Aid at my desk, which I brought in a small thermos. I was trying to be, like the other workers in my soul-deadening position, grateful for the opportunity to work for such a benevolent corporation. And drinking the Kool-Aid did indeed help, though it's impossible to say how much of this was real acceptance of my lot and how much was a mere sugar high. My passion for upgrade sales was applauded, when the supervisor saw me vigorously putting my foot down again and again, stomping the carpet as I spoke into the headset. The supervisor said he was happy to see me be more passionate, "but tone it down a little," so on future calls I dropped my voice a half octave. The customers liked this new voice, and soon I had the leading numbers on my team.

My wife was ecstatic. This meant an easier career path, a bigger bonus. "You're like a whole new person," she beamed, and pulled me into the bedroom, where I tried not to be bothered by how much me being someone else excited her.

When the baby came, I was with her at the hospital with a mouthful of bullets clenched between my teeth. My wife by then had discovered my habit, and accepted it as one of my stranger but more innocuous shortcomings. As she pushed, and screamed, and cried tears of fear and anger and joy, I remained silent, eyes shut, jaw afire with the strain from biting down so hard. I knew I couldn't handle what would be waiting when I opened my eyes. The most important piece of me out there in the world, screaming.

My wife's screams seemed far away, tamped down by the pain in my jaw, then all of a sudden they were up close, right beyond the thin veil my eyelids formed between me and her. The room was filled with the smell of her fluids, and machines beeping, and the stink of sanitation chemicals, and nurses swapping jargon with the doctor. I wondered what would happen if I never opened my eyes again. Like a vow of silence, a sort of celibacy. A vow of blindness. Would my wife lead me through the world by the hand? Would I come to know her face by a particular curvature of bone against my fingers? This, maybe, would not be so bad. I would turn a blind eye, turn both blind eyes. Four senses were more than enough to have to handle.

On the other side of my eyelids there was the shriek of a newborn child. Instinctively, I opened my eyes.

Consider It Saved

IT'S FIVE O'CLOCK ON Christmas evening, and I'm sipping eggnog with my ex-fiancé's whole family. Jan's adopted kid brother is on the floor, tearing violent handfuls of wrapping paper and letting them fall. Her mother, Helen, rests her hand on her husband's thigh and watches the kid with a smile. She just beat cancer. When she thinks no one's looking, I catch her feeling the place where her left breast used to be.

They don't know Jan dumped me three weeks ago.

"Honey?" she says to me. "Will you hand me the scissors?"

She snips the ribbon on the present I gave her and pops open the little black box. It's a pair of earrings she originally saw airborne, when I threw them at the wall. She'd just told me she was leaving me for our friend Lily, in a voice so cold and well-rehearsed it was like reading a block of text.

Now she squeezes my knee. "Honey, they're perfect." I shut my eyes and feel her fingertips linger.

This is the first time we've seen Helen since she found out she was fine again, after months of lost hair and panicked trips to the bathroom. I was the one Jan's dad first told. It was the night of our fight. She had locked herself in the bathroom, her cell phone buzzing incessantly on the nightstand until I picked it up. I stopped beating the heel of my palm against the bathroom door. I'd never heard a man Harry's age cry.

When she came out, I told her the news. We cried and hugged and hatched the big plan not to ruin Christmas.

Her folks live on a beef farm outside Omaha. The first few hours of the day, I helped her dad with the chores. We moved bales of hay to the feeders for the cattle and used a sledgehammer to crack the layer of ice covering the pond so they could drink. The cold wind rippled over the white, lifeless landscape. Harry told me how excited Jan had been watching him blow the creek open with dynamite when she was a child, begging for him to do it again. When we came back inside, Helen brushed away the icicles dangling from his beard and gave me a cup of hot cocoa.

After we open presents, Harry shows me his collection of deer rifles for the millionth time. I nod along, pretending to understand the gun lingo he uses. He runs a clean rag across his favorite and tells me how glad he is I could come this year. When we get back to the kitchen, Harry Jr.'s setting the table.

Before dinner, we hold hands and say grace. I swear I feel Jan's heartbeat through her fingers. I peek out during the prayer, and Jr.'s got his eyes open too. I cross my eyes and stick out my tongue. He giggles.

Harry clears his throat. "For food and family," he says. "Amen."

"Amen," we say.

We stuff ourselves silly: great gobs of gravy heaped on mashed potatoes and turkey, green bean casserole made with real cream, lettuce wedges with grape tomatoes and ranch dressing. We told Helen we'd cook, or at least bring something from Bostón Market, but she wouldn't hear of it. Best way to celebrate she could think of was cooking for her family.

Jan fiddles with her left earring. I ask her if there's something wrong. She shakes her head impatiently, ignoring my question. She asks Helen how she's feeling.

Helen puts her fork down and leans back. Her hair's just now coming in again, a layer of thin gray fuzz stretched over her skull. "That's the only thing anyone's asked me in months," she says. "Who cares? I'm old. I'm supposed to hurt. How are you two? Have you set the date yet?"

Jan taps the table impatiently with the tines of her fork. "I told you, we're waiting until we finish school."

"You'd be surprised how much it takes to plan a wedding," Helen says. There's an impatience in her words I know bites at Jan.

"I know, Mother."

Helen leans in close to Jr. "I'm starting to think you'll be married before those two."

The kid makes a puking sound. "No kidding," Sr. mutters.

"Excuse me," Jan says. She talks the way you might to a stranger blocking your path. She gets up and grabs her purse. I hear her phone buzz in the little pocket just inside, rattling her change. "I need to take this."

Got to be Lily. I tear off some more turkey and try to remember if there was a time she'd interrupt a family dinner to take my call.

Jr. says he wants coffee with his pie, so he can be like me. It's just about more than I can take. Helen winks in my direction. She goes to the kitchen to check if there's any instant decaf.

Harry asks how I think final exams went. I shake my head. I spent finals week drinking beer with breakfast and blasting sad music from my dorm room speakers. It doesn't look good. I excuse myself, and wander off to find Jan.

She's outside the guest bedroom, where we'll sleep tonight. Her smile breaks when she sees me. She holds a single index finger up at me. "I have to go," she says into the phone.

"Me too," she says. I wince.

"It's the middle of goddamn dinner," I hiss as she hangs up the phone.

"Don't curse at me."

"They'll know something's up."

"I'm sorry," she says. "We just wanted to talk two seconds. It's Christmas."

I shut my eyes. "I don't want to hear this."

I feel her hand on my shoulder. "I'm sorry."

"You're embarrassing us."

"Why should I be embarrassed? It's my family."

Her words clamp my throat like a vise. I open my eyes. "Right," I say. "But how do you think they'd react if they knew what I know?"

Her voice softens, like it used to with Jr. when she cooed at him as a baby. "Hey—"

"Dessert is getting cold," I say.

Helen picks up her fork and looks down at her plate, smiling. There's a piece of cinnamon apple pie looking back up at her, topped with a big dollop of vanilla bean ice cream.

"The thing I missed most," she says, "was my taste buds. Chemo made everything taste the way IV tubes smell."

Harry curls his fingers through those of his wife. "Take the first bite, honey. You deserve it."

Jan's phone buzzes in her purse. I poke her in the side and mouth at her, *Turn that thing off.*

Don't tell me what to do.

You're being rude.

I'm not going to answer!

She steps on the toe of my shoe. I slap the table in frustration and everyone looks at me, startled. I clear my throat.

"Sorry," I say. I smile. I take one of Jan's hands from her lap, where they are wringing each other frantically.

Harry stands up. "Jr., let's get you an extra scoop of ice cream," he says.

When he leaves the room, Helen swallows her bite and dabs a cloth napkin against her lips. "You two are acting strange," she says.

Jan sighs extravagantly. "Mom, we've got something to tell you."

I put my arm around Jan and give her a hard, sloppy kiss on the cheek. "We're getting married in August," I say. "We just didn't want to steal your thunder." I take a deep, petulant swig of eggnog.

"Oh, that's wonderful!" Helen says. She claps her hands together, and stands up to get Harry. Jan sits white-faced with shock and bewilderment.

I can't stand cigars, but when Harry offers me one I take it. He came to me first, I noticed: the kid scampered back from the kitchen to jump up into Jan's arms, but Harry crossed to me and gave me one of his hugs where it's so tight you'd think his thin arms might just snap off. He whispered he was so happy, and I peered over his shoulder, miles deep into Jan's worried eyes, and smiled.

"Save the date, Harry," I told him.

"Consider it saved," he said.

Now I'm beside him, winter air slicing in through the cracked window as I put the cigar to my lips. My hand shakes. The end sizzles. There's a burning sensation on the roof of my mouth when I suck the smoke in.

Jan's on the floor, cross-legged and texting Lily. Jr.'s beside her, rolling the wheels of his new dump truck in deep furrows through the carpet. Helen's telling us how she added sour cream to the piecrust dough this time. Everyone's all smiles except Jan. Helen asks if we've thought about the venue yet. "We can do it here," she says, "if you want to push the date back a bit. The garden flowers are beautiful in spring."

"Oh, no," I say. I puff my cigar. "We don't want to wait any longer. Do we, honey?"

Jan puts her phone down. She grins daggers at me. "Of course not. Honey."

"Real traditional," I'm saying. My thoughts swirl like the rocks in my brandy glass. "In a church with one of those, one of those pointy things, a steeple?

"*Honey*," Jan says. "Maybe you should take it easy."

I burp. "And a white dress."

Helen laughs. "Who's going to wear that?"

I laugh too. In a few minutes, Helen asks us to pose for a picture. She motions for us all to scoot together. I pull Jan into my lap, and rest my hand on hers. I give her a kiss on the cheek.

"Come on," I say. "It's a party."

She turns her head and looks at me for a sec, then rolls her eyes. She turns back to Helen.

"Cheese," she says.

Between pictures, I slide my fingers into hers and shut my eyes. I feel her muscles tense, then relax. I picture my hands running up beneath her shirt, then under her beltline, the dip where her stomach ends. I start to get hard. I nestle my nose into her hair, feel my breath warm against her neck. I breathe deep, my lips a millimeter away from her skin.

After the final photo, she sits back down on the floor with Jr.

Just after sunset, as the last bits of red light fragment through the trees that line the farm's edge, I see a family of deer hop from the tall stalks of corn into the woods for the night. I call Jr. over to point them out, but they're gone by the time I lift him up to see. I swallow the last finger of my drink and cough against the burning at the back of my throat. "I wanted you to see," I croak. I feel dumbfounded. I don't know where to put my hands. I turn to the others. "I wanted him to see!" I say.

"Honey," Jan says. "Sit down. You're drunk."

Sr. laughs. "So what if the boy's a bit drunk? It's just us."

Helen shushes him.

I sit down. "So what if I am," I repeat. The words feel strange on my tongue. I say them again and again. I watch Jan, texting furiously. There's a dirty smile at the corners of her lips and eyes. Here we are with her parents, for God's sake.

"Jan's got friends getting married," I say suddenly, like I just thought of it. "Brad and Jason. They're on their way to Vegas right now. While we're celebrating Christmas."

Jan's looking real hard at her hand, at a speck of fingernail polish that's chipped away.

Harry pulls at his mustache. "Whole country's going to hell," he says. "A wedding. My God."

"Quiet, you two," Helen says. "You'll make me sick."

Jan stands up. I'm leaned way back in my chair now, and she looks so beautiful I could get on my knees and beg for just one kiss. There's hate in her eyes, though. It must have been there all day, just waiting to claw its way up to the surface.

"I'm going to put Jr. to bed," she says. "And then I'm going to bed myself."

"Wait up for me," I say.

"No, thank you. You three have your fun."

I try to stand up, but my feet won't cooperate.

"What, no kiss?" I say. The words slip away from me unintended, and I picture myself trying to grab them back with all my strength. She's already gone, clambering up the narrow stairs to her old room.

In an hour or so, when the air coming in through the cracked window has turned to a cold rough as sandpaper, Helen stands up and kisses Harry and me good night. She thanks me for coming. I hug her delicately, not sure how fragile she is, trying not to touch my chest to hers.

She laughs. She says, "Cancer's not contagious, you know." When she pulls away, I tell her how proud I am of her for making it through the last year. I wipe at my eyes drunkenly while I say it. I want to tell her to wait just a few minutes, stay with me just a little longer. She kisses me once more on the cheek before going up to bed. "Take it easy, son," she says.

Harry and I throw some wood into the fireplace, and shove handfuls of newspaper between the cracks. I light them and watch the ink-colored smoke drift up the chimney as I warm my hands.

"Did Jan ever tell you about Jr.'s parents?" he asks me. He's ashing his cigar on the floor now, a thoughtful smile on his face, just begging Helen to scold him in the morning.

"Only that they were friends of yours," I say. "That they named him after you."

He nods. "I knew Bill from when I used to work part-time at the rubber factory. He was twenty years younger, but those things don't matter when you're working that close. I helped him open his bar, he made me godfather. Then one day he and his wife got T-boned running a stop sign on a road outside Waverly."

"Jesus," I say.

He looks down somberly into his half-empty glass. "Actually," he says, "Bill's grandfather was named Harold." He clears his throat. "I guess we just thought Jr. would like being named after me better."

"Are you going to tell him when he's older?"

"Are you crazy? Jan doesn't even know. This is just between us boys. He's my kid now. Bill's gone. The story's changed."

I say nothing. My head's clearer now, drying up like a damp rag that's been wrung out and hung on the line, and I don't like this new secret. Harry and I sit and watch the fire, the flames lapping at the logs so they sizzle and snap like popcorn in oil. When Harry drifts off to sleep, fingers still curled around a glass of watery brandy, I gently tap his cigar out on the hearth and go upstairs.

I shut the door as quietly as I can behind me, not wanting to wake anyone. Jan's lying on the bed, flipping through a magazine.

I sit down next to her. "Hey. Hey, I'm sorry. That was so far out of line."

I touch her leg gently through the covers. "I acted like a jackass all day."

She nods emphatically.

I move my hand away and look at the dresser. It's cluttered with old compact discs, crumpled pink tissue paper, and a tube of black lipstick from her high school goth phase. In all the years since she left home, her parents haven't moved a thing.

"We shouldn't have come," she's saying. "I shouldn't have asked you to."

"I'm glad we did. It's always nice here."

"Nice? Hmm."

"How's Lily?" I ask.

She doesn't answer for a moment. "Good," she says finally.

I swallow hard, vaguely aroused and infuriated by the picture of them together that flits across my brain. "Good," I say. I take off my jeans, remembering how self-conscious I was the first time I undressed in front of her. I slide under the covers. Harry's snores rumble up through the floorboards, and the TV blares news in Helen's bedroom up the hall. I click off the light and stare up into the pitch-black air. This is the last time I'll fall asleep beside her, I realize.

"Was there anything I could have done?" I ask.

She pauses for a beat. "No," she says. I don't press her. I shut my eyes and try to believe it.

Outside, the cold air whips through the frozen cornfields. Tree branches tap against the window. I picture an August wedding, filled with light and blooming flowers, Jan in a white dress dancing with me in a church garden. The roar of the wind brings my mind back to the farm, to the poor cattle feeding on dead corn stalks and half-frozen water, then huddling up for a night in the barn. The roof creaking under the weight of the snow. It needs a new one, I know, but Harry can't afford that. He'll be up there alone come spring, cattle lowing below, patching it once more for the coming winter.

Breath

RODNEY AND I BELIEVED if we held our breath too long we might die. We spent our afternoons up on his roof, taking turns. The roof faced nothing but a big tree, so no one ever saw. We'd time each other on the stopwatch I stole from school, and Rodney would always say something like, "If I get a minute thirty, you got to kiss my shoe." Or bet me: "More than two minutes, that means my mom's coming back."

My mom had told me not to play with Rodney after I stepped on an upturned nail in his dad's work shed. His hair was greasy and he smelled like talcum powder. Years later we'd lose touch after he fell hard into drugs. But Rodney had the lungs of a whale. He'd go a minute thirty at least, then his eyes would roll back in his head. I knew he was putting me on, but still, every time, I'd hunch over him in a panic, slapping color into his cheeks until he opened his eyes. He told me stories about the things he saw: tunnels of light, dead relatives in robes, animals assembled from spare car parts, women with forked tongues. "That was a close one," he'd say. "I almost didn't make it back." But he always did, and that was the point, at least back then. That there was nothing you couldn't come back from.

All the Wild

"IS IT ALWAYS SO BORING?" I asked my brother. It was hunting season, and we were sitting outside on a pair of old buckets we'd used to carry our blankets and ammo. There was plenty of gunfire in the distance, but our own rifles rested unused against their respective trees. We'd been waiting there for hours in that cold strip of woods for a deer to wander through our line of sight.

"Look around, man," Mick said. He waved his hand in a broad motion, a motion meant to indicate the whole world laid bare before us. "You're out in the thick of it. This is what the world is. Trees, patience, light. You want something from it, you have to wait."

More minutes passed. I fished some hardboiled eggs and bacon from the sack Mom had packed. I took a bite of egg and swallowed dryly. It needed salt. "I don't think you answered my question," I said.

Mick sighed. "Yeah," he said, "it's always this boring. Don't tell Mom. Dad and I usually play cards, but I didn't bring any."

After several seasons of bad luck hunting, that year my dad had decided he was done. He'd sat me and Mick and Mom down at our kitchen table and said he wouldn't be going out that year, he just couldn't justify the time away from the restaurant. You would have thought he'd told us we were going to be giving up electricity and living like the Amish.

"But you have to go!" I said. "I'm only thirteen!" Nebraska state law said I needed an adult with me to hunt. And I'd heard from Mick that you didn't want to be the one boy in the grade who didn't go out hunting. No one was so merciless as middle school girls.

"So this is what it's come to," my mother said to my father. "I'm to raise two kids who can't even shoot a gun."

"We've talked about this," my father said.

"I shouldn't be surprised," she muttered, "with a husband who hasn't shot anything in years."

This was my mother's way of arguing, like she was talking to herself, even when we were all around. It was no surprise she objected. Hunting was sacred to her. All the men in her life had always gone. The way you hollowed out a deer after a kill and the entrails lay there in the field, steaming—it said everything about life and death she didn't know how to say.

"Why don't I take Graham?" Mick asked. "I'll borrow the car and drive us out there. We can take the cell phone. If we get anything, we'll call Dad and he can come out and say he was with us."

I frowned at Mick's wording. *We can go together*, he could have said, instead of *Why don't I take him?* But that was me, Graham. I hated the name. The other kids called me Cracker, though we were all equally white.

"Will that make you happy?" Dad asked Mom.

Mom said yes, it would, though we all knew it would not.

• • •

Back then, people had a hard time believing me and Mick were brothers. Even at sixteen, Mick was built like the trunk of a redwood tree. His rough hands looked made for laying brick, all deep lines and cracked skin. Meanwhile my hands were unlined and delicate as a spring day. I was tall for my age but scrawny, the jumpy type of kid you could push over with a feather. I was, Mick informed me when I turned ten, a city slicker at heart. I couldn't help but agree. I was quick to tears, and I disliked the cold small-town air. It made my eyes itch. In my free time I did crossword puzzles and math problems. Hunting was, I knew, Mick and Mom's way of schooling me in the ways of the small town. The season before Mick had shot a buck big enough to fill our freezer for the better part of a year, and I was sure anything less on my part would be considered disappointing, if not unexpected.

I felt the same way around Mick that I felt around most adults back then, at least the men, and many of the kids my own age: namely, that they just didn't know what to do with me. I was a child in Nebraska, a *boy* for Christ's sake, who didn't like football or raising livestock or growing vegetables for the county fair.

The spot we hunted was on a farm that belonged to my Dad's friend Harold, in a line of trees between Harold's farm and the next one. Harold had only lived there a few months, and he was uneasy at first about the two of us being out on his land unsupervised. My dad had convinced him we were mature for our age.

In the middle of the trees ran a muddy, half-frozen stream. Around us was the sound of trickling water and the crackle of squirrels scurrying through the trees overhead.

"You made too much noise walking in," Mick told me. "That's why we haven't seen anything."

"Please," I said. "The way you drive, we'll be lucky if you didn't scare off every deer in the county."

We sat in silence for a while. I nodded off with my head against a tree. We'd had to get up early to be in our spot by sunrise.

"You think Mom will let us keep the meat this year?" I asked Mick when I woke up. The year before Dad and her fought about how much she'd given away. Practically every time she'd gone to a friend's house she'd brought some sausage or some venison as a gift. Dad said it wasn't fair to the kids, we loved the deer meat. But even I knew it was also about money. The restaurant we owned wasn't doing that well, and giving away perfectly good food wasn't going to help things.

Mick said he didn't know.

Another beat of silence.

"I almost don't want to get anything," I said. "If we do Mom's just going to make Dad feel bad. 'See, look at all that meat we almost missed out on!'"

"Of course you want to get something," Mick said. "Don't be a pussy."

Mick pulled a pack of Marlboro Reds out of his pocket. He'd bought it from a friend who worked evening shifts at the gas station, a friend who was known to sell things to people cheap. Forties, liquor—you name it. Even toilet paper, if you asked him right. His dad owned the place, but was bad with numbers. Inventory was a constant confusion, whether his son was stealing or not.

So I smoked my first cigarette with Mick, out there in the trees. I hated the taste but liked the rush of it. The invincible feeling the buzz gave me. I grew four feet in an instant, stood tall over the world, death held in breath-sized chunks between my fingers. The burn in my lungs, in the air. I finished it quick and asked for another. Mick laughed. "No, you don't smoke them like that. Sit and wait a while. You won't buzz again if you don't wait."

So while we waited I made up a game where we each picked a person from town to describe with one-sentence clues, and the other one guessed. It didn't take long for the game to get mean. This person wears the world's worst hairpiece. This woman has whiskers like a cat. This kid's bottom teeth are all sideways. This kid sucked his thumb until third grade.

Then Mick made a pick that made me mad. This was always the thing with Mick, the thing with older brothers. They lift you up to their level just long enough to throw you down in the mud.

"This kid's as jumpy as a grasshopper," he said. When I said I didn't know, he went on. "This kid wet the bed till age six . . . This kid's so bland his nickname suits him . . . This kid's delicate as a newborn kitten."

"I don't want to play anymore," I said.

"Come on," he said, smiling. "*Guess.*"

I stood up. "I'm going to go take a leak." I took the cigarettes and the pack of matches and walked off into the cornfield.

The piss puddled in the dirt by a row of corn, steaming. After I zipped myself back up I lit a cigarette, tossed the match on the ground, and headed back toward the road. I had half a mind to just walk home. It would take a while, but I was done with hunting. I could always just go back to school the next day and lie, say I already shot something.

On my way back I had to pass Harold's house, and a woman I assumed was his wife came out onto the back porch to say hello. She wore a blue and white checkered shirt and had blond hair pulled back in a bun. I was lucky to have just ground out my cigarette beneath my heel. She looked like the type who would tell Mom. I felt my cheeks turn red as she looked me up and down. She was very pretty.

She crossed her arms in the cold. "You must be Graham," she said. "Where's your brother? You're not out here by yourself, are you?"

"I wish," I said. I spat on the ground. It was the angriest, manliest gesture I could think of.

I watched Betty try to suppress a smile. That made me all the more angry.

"I don't even want to be here!" I shouted suddenly. "Mom made me come." This was a thing I hadn't realized until then. In a house like mine, you didn't always know a thing until you yelled it at somebody.

Betty looked startled. "Oh," she said. "Um. Do you want to come inside?" She said it in a way like she was more than a little terrified at the idea. But I nodded yes and followed her in.

• • •

Betty led me to the kitchen table and pulled a chair out for me. "You want anything?" She asked. "A pop? Some milk? I think I have a slice of pie." She opened the refrigerator door and stared in. As she bent down to look I took a strong interest in the view I had. Since the summer before when I'd started discovering the things my body was capable of, I had gotten very good at recording images like this for future use.

I didn't know what to say, so I didn't say anything. My mind was balled up with anger at Mick and fatigue from the early morning. When I didn't respond Betty set a slice of pie and some milk in front of me. "Eat this," she said. "You'll feel better."

I picked up the fork and shoveled a bite into my mouth. It was so cold it made my eyes water, but it was good. She'd put in cinnamon and you could tell the apples were fresh. This was a woman who made homemade crust. Hell, she probably picked the apples herself.

Betty took a seat across from me and folded her hands on the table. She had a vibrant beauty that clashed with her surroundings. "You're having a bad time out here," she said.

I nodded. I took another bite of pie. I couldn't remember the last time Mom had made me pie. Usually she slapped my hand away. *Cut it out, Graham, that's for the customers.*

"I'm sorry I yelled," I said. "I'm short on sleep."

"Do you want me to call your mom? I bet she can come get you."

I shook my head. "No, she'll make me go back to school."

"I liked school when I was your age."

"Yeah. I think that's a girl thing."

She laughed. "So what's the boy thing, waking up at six in the morning to go sit in a cold field? Doesn't sound like fun to me."

"No, I guess not."

I looked around the little house. It was all immaculate. White countertops scrubbed clean, spotless linoleum, a water bowl by the kitchen sink for some animal that looking around you'd swear never shed. I could see into the living room at an angle. There was a TV with rabbit ears, and a small shelf full of books. "Where are you coming from?" I asked her.

"I'm from Kansas City, originally," she said. "Harold grew up around here. It was always a dream of his to come back and buy a farm. We just got here a few months ago."

I shook my head. "Once I escape," I said, "I'm never coming back."

"Oh, it's not so bad," she said. But the way she looked around the little house as she said it, as if searching for some sort of evidence, made me think she wasn't so sure.

We decided to let Mick sit out in the field a while and worry. At least I wanted to think he was worried. Let him think I walked on home to cry to Mom. Let him think he had a whole heap of trouble waiting for him at home. I was enjoying my time with Betty. It felt strangely invasive to be inside someone else's home, invasive in an exciting way, eating their food and watching their TV. But there was something sad about it too, this woman all alone with nothing to do until her husband got home. Their harvest was all done, and Harold was up at a neighbor's farm helping out for some extra cash.

A little before sunset I headed back out to find Mick and get my rifle. Sunset was best for spotting deer, I'd heard. It's when they wake up and maybe feel a bit hungry, a bit thirsty. Head out for a tasty nibble of corn from the stalks, or to wet their snouts in the river. We could shoot until a half hour after the sun went down. I walked quiet as I could back to our spot in the trees, careful to avoid fallen cornhusks.

Mick heard me coming up behind him. He craned his head around. "Look who it is," he whispered, also careful not to make too much noise.

"Go to hell," I said. I sat down. Mick had his gun across his lap. I left mine leaning against the tree.

"Where you been?"

"None of your business," I whispered back. "You killed anything yet?"

"Sure. Loads of 'em. Look at all these dead deer."

He motioned at the empty ground in front of us.

"Seen anything at least?"

He shook his head. "Around four I got bored and shot up a fence post pretty good."

"Great," I said. "Maybe we can mount that and put it on the wall."

The woods grew darker.

"I was worried you went home," Mick said.

"Not worried enough to go looking."

He blew warm air into his hands. He looked like he wanted to say something. The air was getting cold again. I put my gloves back on and pulled a spare blanket out of the bucket and pulled it up onto my lap. The deep yellow sun touched down on the horizon line. The air was hazy with cold dust, blowing off of the fields, so that the sun appeared to shimmer. I felt the grit in my eyes and squinted out at it, biting at a flap of dead skin hanging from my lip. It had started to smell like snow. Like hell would I be back the next day if it started to snow, I thought.

About fifty yards out from where our line of trees curved westward and shot off onto the neighboring land, something stepped out into the field. Something big, with two littler somethings trailing behind. The rack on the one in front rose up into the sky.

"Mick," I whispered.

"I see it."

He shouldered his rifle and looked through the scope. Mine was leaning against the tree. I was terrified to move for it. I didn't want to attract the deer's attention. Them there in front of me, it seemed a thing delicate as a smoke ring. I was afraid if I breathed too hard they might disappear.

A sudden flush of indignation filled me. Son of a bitch, I thought. Mick's going to get the kill out of sheer dumb luck, having his rifle on his lap. Easy as shooting up a fence post.

"Well," I whispered, "go on already." But Mick just sat there, scope to his eye. In the field, the deer moseyed along the rows of corn. A buck and a doe and a fawn. A moment later, Mick lowered his gun. Something was churning behind his eyes and lips. I saw a trembling there. "I don't know," he said.

"What don't you know?" I hissed, a little too loud. "Shoot it already."

The buck stopped and looked in our direction. The other deer stopped too and all of a sudden the whole world was stock-still, looking at us, what we were going to do.

"It's a family," Mick said. "A mother and a father and a fawn."

What's that got to do with anything? I thought wildly. Slowly, looking the buck dead in the face, I leaned forward on my bucket and wrapped my fingers around the barrel of my rifle. Then I leaned slowly back, taking the rifle with me. *There you go, be still now*, I thought at the deer. I put the stock to my shoulder and peered out through the scope.

He was right, I supposed. I centered the crosshairs on the baby deer. It was small enough that it couldn't be out on its own. I drifted the crosshairs to the right, over the ridge of the mother's spine. She was a medium-sized doe, nothing special. Then the buck. I counted three points on each antler. He was standing with his great brown body perpendicular to us, his head craned our way, watching my every move. I trained my crosshairs on his heart and flipped the safety.

"He's a father," Mick whispered. There was something weak and raw in his voice. I took one deep, calm breath. Then I pulled the trigger.

There was a great boom and I felt the gun jump back against my shoulder. Without leaning away from the scope I pulled the bolt back to eject the casing and sent another one into the chamber. It wasn't necessary. I watched the animals scatter off through the field. The doe first, followed by the fawn. The buck bounded forward a few steps, then fell down into the corn where we couldn't see him anymore.

I let out a hoot of joy. "I got him!" I said. I stood up and put the safety on and slung the gun back over my shoulder. I smacked Mick on the back. He looked stunned.

"Buck up," I said, not intending the pun but not exactly minding it either. I think I saw him wince. I grabbed my rifle and a bucket of supplies and took off. After a moment, I heard his footsteps trailing behind.

The buck was on the other side of the stream, so I had to go down onto the muddy bank and leap across it. There was a sucking sound beneath my boots but I barely noticed. I was full of light, even as it faded from the field. The whole forest and everything in it, all the wild earth, it was all for me.

We found the buck on the ground on his side, head cocked back at an impossible angle. It looked like he'd hit the ground still breathing, judging by the bloodied scuff marks in the dirt, then started to kick his legs and scooted back a few feet across the ground. His great body was stretched back forever in one deep breath. He'd taken half a dozen stalks of corn with him, cracked down in his final fight with the darkness falling around him. It was a good, clean kill, I saw with pride. Right through the chest.

I stood there a moment, admiring my handiwork in the fading light. "We've got to call Dad," Mick said beside me. "He'll have to say he was here. You need an adult present."

"Yeah, all right, call him then." I laid my gun down in the dirt.

Mick took the cell phone out of his pocket and punched in the number for the restaurant. My fingers and lips were numb with cold. I half listened to Mick talking to Dad, stuttering out the words, and put my tag on the thing's ear. Mick must be in awe of me, I thought. A six-point buck my first year. That will show him. Everyone else, too.

"He's an ugly one, huh?" Mick said quietly as he hung up the phone. He motioned with his gloved hand at the antlers. One of the tips was cracked.

"You don't get that big without having some fight in you."

"Well, Dad's on his way. He's got to call around to find a ride out here."

I looked over at my brother. He was holding his scarf to his mouth, staring down at the dead deer.

"It's getting dark," I said.

"Yeah."

"We won't have any light to dress him by."

"Dad's on his way."

I took a couple deep breaths, real attentive to the cold air surging in and out of me, looking at the red hole torn into the buck's lungs. I felt like a lucid dream, all power. "We won't have any light," I said. "And the damn thing's bleeding on my meat."

I left Mick standing there, staring dumbly at the thing, and I set off back to the line of trees to find a good stick. I saw a decent branch right away and jumped and grabbed it with both hands, pulling down with all my weight. It snapped off. Then I broke it again over my knee. I carried the better half back to Mick.

"Help me move it," I said.

"What for?"

"We've got to dress it while there's still light. Help me turn it on its back."

"Like hell."

"Come on, the meat will spoil." I got down on the ground and started tugging at it. It was impossibly heavy. All dead weight. I grabbed its front hooves and back hooves all together and pulled. It barely moved an inch. I looked up at Mick and he shook his head. Something was wrong with him. He looked sick. I tugged at the thing's feet some more. I rose to mine and heaved with all my strength, enough to slide the thing off the flattened stalks of corn and onto the dirt. I got down on my knees and put my hands under it. Its fur was still warm. I pulled up with everything I had, feeling a deep burn in my muscles, but nothing happened. "Come on!" I shouted at Mick, and after a moment he got down on his knees and helped. The thing slumped over onto its back, legs splayed out. I looked up at its head and the antlers were tracing new lines in the dirt. Its eyes were black. Its lips were slightly parted, showing its soft pink tongue and yellow nubby teeth. I put the branch I'd grabbed between its hind legs, propping them open wide, and wiped the sweat off my forehead with the back of my sleeve.

I pulled a flashlight out of the bucket and clicked it on. I handed it to Mick. "Hold that," I said. Then I grabbed the buck knife and flipped it open.

This was a thing I'd seen my dad do a couple times, when I'd ridden my bike out after school to meet Mick and him during deer season. He would always gut Mick's kills, and explain himself as he did it. He said it was best done right away, otherwise you could lose meat. I put the blade tip to the animal's fur just below the rib cage. I pressed against it gradually, until there was a release of pressure and it slid in. Then I started carving downward. There was a sound like tearing fabric. The thing opened up and in the beam of the flashlight Mick held I saw steam rising from the hole I'd made. I cut around the genitals and pulled out the bladder, slicing at the top as I did. Then together we rolled the buck onto his side and watched his organs spill out. I helped them out with my hand, slicing gently at the connections there were between them and the rest of the carcass. The wet organs were slippery in my hand. "Keep the light still," I told Mick. I looked up and he wasn't even looking at me. His eyes were off at the edge of the field.

"Graham," he said queasily. I followed his eyes. There at the edge of the field on the south side, along another line of trees, was the fawn, watching me work. I stood up and looked at him. Suddenly burning at him, the brazenness. Wasn't he scared of me? I wiped at my runny nose with the back of my forearm because my hands were covered in blood. "Go on!" I shouted. The thing didn't move. I picked up my gun.

"Jesus, Graham, no, he's just a kid," Mick said. He grabbed the gun from me, careful to keep the barrel pointed away, off into the trees. He wiped the blood off the stock with the sleeve of his flannel. His eyes searched mine the way you'd search the wreckage of a battlefield. "What's the matter with you?" he said.

I got back down on the ground to scoop the rest of the blood out of my buck. "I was only going to scare him is all," I said. I wondered idly if that was true. There wasn't much on my mind when I grabbed the gun, to be honest. Just a flash of white-hot power and rage mixed up into a little ball, and that dumb deer staring at me with those hurt eyes.

"Just hold the damn light already," I said. "And blast a couple shots into the air to get that fawn out of here."

• • •

By the time Dad got there the field was pitch-black. We heard him calling to us from the other side of the stream. "Over here!" Mick called. He waved his arms in the air, though there was no way Dad could see. A flashlight beam shot dimly through the trees, breaking into pieces between the trunks. "Hell of a kill," he said when he found us and trained the flashlight on the deer. He frowned. "You could have waited to gut it. I would have helped you."

"I didn't know when you'd get here," I said.

Dad got down on his knees and peered into its parted torso with his flashlight, pulling on one of its legs to open it up. "You shouldn't have done that without me," he said. "You could have ruined the meat." I clenched my fist at my side. Was he being serious right now? I felt like I deserved a gold medal in deer dressing. He knew how easy it was to pop the bladder or puncture the stomach wall, and I'd done neither. He stood up and scratched at his beard. "I guess we better go talk to the Neukirchs. You shot the thing off Harold's land. If they ask, say you shot him back there and he ran through to the other side."

My dad shined the flashlight beam on me and laughed. "You look like one of your zombie shows," he said. Blood covered my shirt and hands.

On the way back to the car, we walked by Betty's house. The lights were on in the living room. I saw her part the blinds to look out at us, traipsing as we were out of the field, the back-porch light shining onto our buckets, our faces, our guns. The blood on my shirt. I grinned at her and waved with my free hand. She drew the blinds closed sharply without smiling back or returning my gesture.

The next Sunday, my mom baked Betty and Harold a pecan pie. She insisted I needed to show some thanks to them for letting me hunt their ground. "Go ask your father to drive you out there," she said. Things at home were tenser than ever. She and Dad weren't speaking. "Your father" was the closest she'd come to saying his name.

The day after I'd shot my deer, we'd decided to sleep in rather than head back out at first light, even though we had another tag Mick could use. Mick said he wasn't feeling well, and anyway we'd made enough noise the night before that it was probably better to give it a day or two for the deer to return. Mom was so thrilled at that point at the glut of meat set to fill our fridge she didn't even make us go to school. She said we deserved a day of rest.

But then that evening Mick said he didn't want to go back out at all. He'd had his fill of freezing his balls off in some field, he said, and anyway the meat from my deer would be plenty. Something in the way he said it, a flash of that uneasiness he'd shown in the field, and I knew it was more than that.

"You're going to let your little brother be the man of the family, then," my mom said. We were at the dinner table, and she'd had some wine with her food. "You and your father. Christ."

This was the first shot fired in a long argument that stretched into the next day and settled into a cold spell between the three of them. Mom wanted Mick to man up, Dad wanted Mom to lay off, Mick wanted to be left alone. I may as well have not been there at all.

So when I went out to bring Betty that pecan pie, it was by myself. Dad wouldn't drive me, said he wanted nothing to do with anything of my mother's, including pie. So I rode my bike, slowly, holding the pie on top of the handlebars with one hand and steering with the other. I may have tried to get out of this errand if I hadn't been eager to see Betty again. That afternoon in her house, it was the first time in a long time I'd felt right at home.

But when she ushered me in, her manner was cold as the air outside. She didn't look at me when she asked if she could get me anything. Harold was with her now, and he shook my hand. "Get the boy some hot cocoa," he said. "Make it with milk."

He and I sat down at the kitchen table. "Your dad said it was a hell of thing, that buck you shot."

I nodded. I pulled out some pictures we'd taken before we drove it to the butcher. There was my deer strapped to the trunk of the car, a thin trickle of blood at its mouth and its great horns intertwined with the luggage rack.

"Hell of a thing," Harold said again, fanning out the pictures. For a moment Betty stood over us, peering down at them, then looked away. There was that uneasiness again at the sight of the deer, the one I'd seen in Mick. My child's mind registered this as a sort of betrayal. My eyes followed her to the stove, where she was heating some milk. Something in my chest tightened like an angry fist. Her back was to me now. It felt like I could wait there my whole life and she would never turn around.

When I got home, Mick was in our room sitting on the edge of his bed, staring down at a biology book. He was taking notes on a yellow legal pad. I asked him what he was doing and he said, "What's it look like I'm doing? Mind your own business."

I lay down on my bed in a huff. He knew I was into all that stuff. Books, math, biology. In his better moments in the past he would tell me to come sit beside him and explain what he was reading best he could. It was way more advanced than what they had me studying in school.

But he didn't do that now. And I got the sense then that lines had been drawn in the sand, and without realizing it I'd drawn a small circle right around myself. I curled up wordlessly on the bed with a black pen and a book of crossword puzzles, waiting for Mom to call us down for dinner.

Snapshots

AT A CERTAIN POINT, I realized I wanted to have children but not to raise them. So I packed up and moved myself to a hotel room across town. My wife, Rosie, sent me pictures in the mail. Our daughter, Cynthia, smiling against the wall, hair in a neat part down the side. Jacob in his crib, face soft and content with some happy dream. *This is what you are missing*, her notes said.

I wasn't sure how she found me. I'd suspended my cell phone service and changed my email address. Nearest I could figure, she had called every hotel in town, asking to be put through to my room and waiting for one that didn't say it had no guest by that name. Two days before the first photo, the phone in my room let out a single sharp, angry ring and fell silent.

She didn't call again, and she didn't come to the hotel. She just sent these pictures, each one stranger than the last. I started to look forward to them, to seeing what she might see fit to send. Here was Jake in his high chair at the kitchen table, orange muck on his face and bib. Cynthia, the part in her hair now mussed, red-faced and screaming in the kitchen, waving a wooden spoon in the air. What a shot, I had to admire. I imagined my wife snapping the photo right then, mid–screaming match, the nerve that took. *This is what you are missing*, the photos still said, red ink scrawled in block letters at the bottom.

Then came one of Rosie leaned back on a heap of pillows, spreading herself open wide, a look of tussled, angry ecstasy on her face. Who's holding the camera? she must have wanted me to wonder. In another she glared out at me, hands at her sides forming fists, nude but for a tampon string hanging out of her.

I eBayed an old camera and walked the hotel grounds with the strap around my neck, snapping pictures. I wanted something to send in return. The ice bucket in my room, plastic liner inside, holding a shallow pool of water from the night before. The laundry room they left open, white sheets spinning, the indifferent Romanian woman there reading a book. The teen at the front desk with acne like spider bites, the piece of carpet with a stain like blood, a dog relieving himself in front of my door. It got so I'd snapped hundreds of these, but nothing seemed to say what I wanted.

I called her just so she could hear my voice, how even it was, how it didn't ask about who held the camera for her.

She sounded sleepy. "Who is it?" she said.

"Me. I thought I should call."

Silence a moment while she considered this.

"The children miss you," she said. "I can't for the life of me tell why."

"And you?"

Here the line started to crackle. I tried to push the end of the cord more firmly into the receiver, thinking the connection was loose. She was saying something, but I couldn't hear. Her voice was like a fighter pilot on the way down, spitting static at me.

"I can't hear," I said. "Are you yelling?"

I put the receiver down to press some buttons on the dock, to fiddle with the cord there. By the time I picked it up again, the line was dead.

"Rosie?" I said. "Rosie?"

I tried to fix it for a long time, plugging and unplugging the jack, shining the number pad with spit, pressing and unpressing the lever that hung it up, but whenever I listened to the line even the dial tone was raspy with static.

I took a picture of the phone to send to her, my way of apology. But then I couldn't tell what it showed, and knew she wouldn't be able to either: a phone fallen to disrepair despite all the best intentions, or a phone that would work just fine if her husband bothered to try it again.

Now Nothing

I WANTED TO SAY, WANTED to insist, that I was a good man. I was three drinks drunk on a mix of strong white wine, pineapple ice cream, and grenadine at a dive bar off the yellow line. They called the drink a terremoto—an "earthquake," for how unsteady the ground felt after you had a couple. I had yet to try to stand.

My then-girlfriend, later-fiancée, now-nothing was at home with her old DVDs of *Sex and the City*. She was also drunk, quite verbally so, but on something thoroughly North American. Whiskey, I think, mixed with Coca-Cola she bought at the botillería around the corner. Lately she'd become impossible, and she said the same of me. We'd been in Chile for three months by then and the culture shock had chewed us all to hell. The language, the different social mores, the lack of air-conditioning. She'd reached the point where she didn't want to go out anymore, said she couldn't go to one more restaurant where she had to keep her purse on her lap or else someone would steal it. I'd started stockpiling take-out menus from nearby restaurants, organized by which ones were most patient with nonnative speakers when you called. We were everywhere baffled, even at home, and when the opportunity arose we tore into each other.

I'd left in a huff after a fight about nothing and now across from me was a chilena named Meryl, after the North American actress. She looked about my age, mid-to-late-twenties. She wore black jeans and had her legs crossed with her ankle on her knee, like a man. I had mistakenly tried to confide in her, and she was now telling me that all men were dogs, worse than dogs. She said she felt sorry for my woman, but not for me. She felt sorry for all women everywhere. Men were impossible, always impossible. Then she told me this story.

When Meryl was younger, she had worked as a street prostitute. From age eighteen she'd spent her weekend evenings in Parque Forestal or on Vicuña Mackenna, finding clients then walking to one of the nearby hoteles de amor that charged hourly.

My god, I said in Spanish. I am so sorry.

I am not one of those men, I added.

She said to shut up and listen.

One day a woman approached Meryl in Parque Forestal. She had blond hair, clearly a gringa. It was winter but you could see her bangs poking out from beneath her hat. Get out of here, Meryl told her. I don't do women.

In broken Spanish the woman said it wasn't for her but for her boyfriend. Her fiancé. She started to cry.

They were standing next to a stone sculpture of a horse, rearing up on its hind legs. There were two other women standing not far off from Meryl, also waiting for customers, but when the gringa started to cry they moved deeper into the park, to another well-lit place untainted by the sound of this woman's sobs. I am weak, the gringa was saying. Why has God made me so weak?

Meryl stayed out of stubbornness, not willing to give up her usual spot, wanting to insist that it be the gringa who left instead. In her start-and-stop Spanish shot through with tears, the gringa started telling Meryl about how her boyfriend had just proposed. He'd bought a cheap ring off the street, promising to buy her a real ring next time they were in the States.

That's where we're from, the States, the woman said. You have to understand, he did not want to, how do you say, be cheated here. We know there is always a special price for gringos.

The gringa tried to laugh. She wiped at her eyes.

All this time Meryl was watching the periphery, scanning for potential customers. She was afraid the woman's blond hair, even mostly covered, would draw attention away from her.

Congratulations, Meryl said, unsure what else the woman might be looking for, hoping this might be the end of it.

No, listen, the gringa said, stepping closer. I am weak. I don't believe him when he tells me things, when he buys me things. I think, what might he be hiding?

Despite herself, Meryl stopped watching the edges of the park and glanced at the woman. She was now very close, close enough to kiss. Her words were hard to follow, jumbled as they were with tears and emotion and misconjugations. But Meryl got the general idea, and soon she was genuinely intrigued.

The woman wanted Meryl to seduce her potential husband. Or rather, in an ideal world—which I must now interject this world surely is not—to attempt to seduce him. To confirm that even if women threw themselves at him, he would turn them away. That the gringa was all he wanted.

I want you to be the opposite of me, the gringa said. Men like women helpless, no? I am not helpless. Do you speak English?

A little.

Do not speak any English. Be helpless.

The gringa had stopped crying. She asked Meryl for a cigarette, and as Meryl leaned in to light it for her she saw an indignant fury in the gringa's eyes under the reflected flame. The gringa took a long, full puff and started to cough.

Be helpless, the gringa said again.

Meryl met the man at a new hipster bar in Lastarria. It had high walls covered in reproductions of ironic art. The waiters wore black aprons and T-shirts of American sports teams. She sat down beside the fiancé at the bar. She'd been shown his picture, and was told he'd be there around nine. He gave English classes down the street, and always stopped for a glass of wine after. He was a plain-looking man with an early gray streak at his temples, but he spoke Spanish well. Almost no accent.

Meryl had learned to act many different ways in front of men. She could only be herself in front of women, but in front of men this was impossible. She was too used to reading their desire and acting accordingly. So it was easy for her to tell the man, blush rising to her cheeks, that she had left her wallet at her office. She was a receptionist there, and the doors were now locked.

I don't know what I'm going to do, she said. I don't have my metro card, I have no way to get home. Would you buy me a glass of wine? It helps me think.

The man bought her a glass of wine. He even offered her his metro card. It only cost a couple thousand pesos. He could always get another. The man was very generous.

Meryl told him her name was Marcela, and said he spoke Spanish well, though too formally to be Chilean. She asked him to tell her about himself. After that he wouldn't shut up. He told her all his big gringo plans. He wanted to start a shelter for the stray dogs on the Santiago streets. He wanted to volunteer-teach the following summer in the poorer regions of the country. Meryl nodded along generously with all his ideas, as if she understood why someone would care so much for the neighborhood dogs, many of which were fat on the scraps people left for them. As if a couple English classes would solve the problems of the poverty-stricken. As he talked he crumpled and uncrumpled the cocktail napkin that had come with his drink. He said he wanted to write a book in English about the aftershocks of the Pinochet regime, to share the voices of the missing and the dead. He was no writer, he said, but there were stories that needed to be told.

They shared several glasses of wine. He asked about the place she said she worked, a copper mining company with locations up and down Chile, but he seemed at a loss for ways to pursue this line of conversation. He did better discussing himself. He waved his hand dismissively when Meryl said thank you, a thousand thank-yous, for the wine. Meryl had a high tolerance for wine. Men liked to watch her drink it, liked to buy it for her, and she knew how to act tipsy, or "happy" as they say in Chile.

After a while the man said he had to get home. Still he made no mention of any fiancée, and Meryl thought that this was a bad sign. She'd begun to root for her gringita, for the idea that two people could belong to each other in a way that wasn't sordid. She wanted this man to politely rebuff her advances, not offer to walk her to the metro and buzz her through, which was what he was now doing.

Outside the metro stop, Meryl leaned against the railing next to the stairs leading down to the train. Above her was a glowing red *M* for metro. Give me a minute, she said. She touched two fingers to her temple. I think I'm drunk, she said.

I'll put you in a cab, the man said. The metro will close soon.

Meryl shook her head. The man touched her shoulder and asked if she was sure. She leaned in and kissed him gently, playfully, on the lips. He said something and started to back away. She gave him another kiss, acting hungrier now, tugging gently at the hair on the back of his head. The man kissed back, just for a moment. Then he pulled away.

For the first time now his Spanish was less sure. He was visibly aroused and stuttered a bit and said he couldn't, he was engaged. He offered again to give her cab money.

Meryl laughed. I don't want your money, weón, I want you. The man turned red and walked away, hands in his pockets.

In a grimy bar many years later, I smiled happily over my drink, though I knew from Meryl's initial comments that the story was not over. There was some spin she would give it, the way a bowler applies spin to his ball so halfway down the lane it veers off at a new angle, toward some less obvious destination. Maybe the point Meryl had extracted from all this was the way the gringa's doubts lingered, the impossibility of ever trusting anyone else. Or that the gringo had a hard-on and in that moment kissed her back, his body betraying him at a biological level, showing its thirst for more than his fiancée.

I was sure that somehow Meryl had missed her own point: that people can be true to each other. I thought of my then-girlfriend, back at our apartment. I wanted to go home and bury myself in the crook of her neck, the hem of her dress, and cry for all the moments we'd ever spent apart, in doubt.

You see, I said, there are good people out there.

She gave me a look of deep disgust. Oye, weón, she said, the story is not finished. I saw that woman again, months later, walking rapidly through Parque Forestal at night. I yelled after her, angrily, and chased her. The gringa tried to run but couldn't run fast enough.

Meryl explained the deal had been that the gringa would pay half up front and half after she did or did not fuck the husband-to-be, a high sum because in all things there is always a higher price for gringos. But the gringa had never returned. Meryl had imagined the gringa had forgot all about the other half of the money when her fiancé had arrived home unsoiled. Perhaps a guilt-filled roll in the sack had wiped her mind and conscience clean. Or perhaps she was so shamed by her doubt that she couldn't bring herself to return to Meryl with the money. Whatever the reason, Meryl was now annoyed. So she grabbed the gringa's sleeve, and the gringa started to cry. Dios mío, she thought, the tears with this one.

But this time the tears wouldn't stop. The gringa sat down on the sidewalk, still crying, looking around like she was unaware how to stand back up. Cars passed on the street. A couple male voices shouted come-ons from half-cracked windows zooming past. Meryl started to back away, to leave the woman there, and now the woman grabbed *her* arm with both hands. Don't leave, she said, please don't leave me. I'm sorry I didn't return. It was too painful.

She explained that when the fiancé arrived home, he said nothing about Meryl or her alias, Marcela. For a while after work he'd sent texts explaining he was at the bar, was going to stay for one more drink, it had been a long day. No mention of anyone else. Then he went silent for some time, almost an hour, before a final text that read simply *Omw*. The gringa's mind swelled with all the possibilities, all the things that might transpire in a lost hour.

When he got home she asked where he had been. Drinking, he said simply. Cell phone reception was weak in the bar. He asked her what was wrong. She locked herself in the bedroom.

The gringa assumed the worst. Why else would he lie? Why that night of all nights would he stay so long at the bar, ignoring her texts? A silence came to sit between them, a silence that began as an ache at the back of her throat and as days passed grew to fill their entire apartment. One night he leaned in to kiss her and she turned away, unable to unimagine his lips intertwined with Meryl's. The gringo exploded. He yelled he did not know what was wrong with her lately. He demanded an explanation and she told him, yelling and pointing a finger into his chest, that she'd sent that chilena there to test him. That he'd failed, obviously, and now he thought things could go on as they had before.

She continued to thump her finger into his chest and the man shoved her, sent her sprawling back. Pain crackled through her tailbone and hands where they hit the floor. Water rushed to her eyes but she willed herself not to cry. She looked up at him, looming. There was a menace to his posture she'd never seen before, his whole body taut like a cord about to snap. She was afraid to move. The way he clenched his fists frightened her. I never fucked that chilena, he said. From her space on the floor she watched him gather a few changes of clothes, and when she finally found her voice she hated herself for begging him to stay.

When I got back home, my then-girlfriend was asleep on the couch. Her face was awash in blue light. On the TV, the episode selection menu hummed the *Sex and the City* theme song. I woke her up and as I did so I told myself it was for her, not for me. That she would want to know I was home, that she would want me to move her into the bedroom to sleep. She didn't ask me where I'd been. She was either afraid of what I would say or trusted me or didn't give a shit anymore anyway. In bed I told her I had missed her, and she started to snore.

When she woke up in the morning, I tried to be better. I tried to open up, let a little light in, tell her what I was feeling instead of sectioning off my little corner of the world apart from her. Sometimes I succeeded and it felt good. But I didn't tell her Meryl's story. I was afraid she'd see through me. I was afraid she'd wonder which one I was, the one who would accept the advances or shun them then hurt her later, more cruelly. We all have rough edges to press into each other. Meryl's story would unmake us, I feared, one way or another.

But I wanted to tell the story to someone. Now I guess I have. Three last lines occur to me. I know they can't all be true.

One. Secrets between people are like infected wounds, needing to be lanced.

Two. It's the truths we withhold that make love possible.

Three. The worst violence in this story is the one I commit here now, in making it about myself.

The So-Called Jacob

IT WAS MY SON'S first day of daycare, and I was waiting in line to retrieve him. I'd arrived a little late, and the line already stretched almost to the door. At the front a bored twenty-something sat behind a desk. A sign nailed to the wall behind her read *Retire su hijo aquí*—get your kid here.

After a while I noticed the guy ahead of me was holding a pink piece of paper with a large, official-looking stamp. I asked him where he got it and if I needed one myself to get my son. He nodded, pointing to a small wood door in the corner. A handwritten note taped to it read *Documentos de paternidad*. "You are new here?" he asked me in English. I wasn't sure what he meant—new at the daycare, new in the country, or maybe something more general, like whether I was born yesterday.

I tried not to let all this strike me as strange. I had moved here with my wife and son for an adventure, with no knowledge of the daily costs of acclimating to a new language, a new culture, a new sense of self. Every small task was a new opportunity for ineptitude. Still, all the expat blogs assured me that just because something was different didn't mean it was bad. Besides, Jacob was probably having the time of his life back there, playing with the other kids, making friends.

So I slumped through the little doorway into a smaller, stuffier room full of tired-eyed parents. Some were in line, some just milling about. Most had brought a magazine or an iPad to pass the time. I asked someone what the line was for, and she pointed to a faded red contraption in the corner like they used to have in pharmacies, with a spool of paper and a numbered slip hanging out like the tongue of an exhausted dog. She explained that after you took a number they eventually called you up to Ventanilla 5 to show your ID, then after that you stood in the line to retrieve your pink piece of paper.

I wanted to say, *Who the hell thought of that?* But my wife had assured me this daycare was the best of the best. So I calmly took a number, leaned against the wall, and waited to be called.

An hour later, back in the first room, I reached the front of the final line. I handed the woman behind the desk my proof of paternity. The room was now almost empty, save for three or four people in line behind me. The tile floor was littered with remnants from those who had passed through: empty cola cans, gum wrappers, a pair of shades, even an empty aguardiente bottle. The woman studied my piece of paper. I smiled. She frowned. Then she went into the back, and a few minutes later brought out Jacob.

At least, she said it was Jacob. She led him out holding his hand, which was weird. My son was very shy for a child of two, and hated holding hands. What's more, he was walking differently, as if his left foot was heavier than his right, and held his jean shorts up by a belt loop.

The woman slid back behind the desk and asked me in perfect English to sign a Receipt of Child Form. I didn't move.

"We just bought those shorts," I told her. "They should fit perfectly."

"Maybe he lost weight," she said.

"In a few hours?" I knelt down, eye to eye with the boy. "Jacob," I said, "how was daycare?"

The face looked like that of my son but the eyes were different, simple brown instead of hazelnut flecked with green. And the hair, before parted to the left because of a cowlick that made something simpler impossible, now lay flat. He didn't answer my question. I stood up.

"This isn't my son," I said.

She nodded, unconcerned, and pulled a piece of paper from her desk drawer. She explained in a terse, well-practiced speech that this was a form acknowledging that I had received *a* child, ID number 3041, but that I was not yet ready to acknowledge he was mine. She showed me the tag on his shirt that confirmed the number. "Take him home. Talk to your wife, if you have a wife. Tomorrow we will straighten this out."

At home, I put him up on the kitchen counter, on display for Daphna. He stood very still, eerily so, but wouldn't talk. I showed her his mud-brown eyes, how his hair lay flat, how slender his waist was. She glanced at her watch and said something about dinner. When I told her about the form I'd filled out, she scolded me.

"We've been over this," she said impatiently. "Things will be different here. Even Jacob. *Especially* Jacob."

In the morning, when I dropped him off at daycare, there was no mention of my confusion the day before. And when I returned to pick him up, I knew to get there early.

The Slabs

THE SUBJECTS ARE IN THEIR rooms with their slabs, and it's Jenna's and my job to watch. There's a hidden camera looking in on each one. All we have to do is press the red button on the console if we see any emergencies. Jenna and I each get a slab too. The buttons and touch screen are disabled. The company wants to see what people will ask these things to do, when they have to ask.

We pass the time making fun of the subjects. There's the husky bald guy who's got the biggest dick you've ever seen and won't stop touching himself. There's the teenager who's constantly sending videos. In one she pulls up her bedspread, pressing her palm against the resistant mattress. She tells the slab, "Caption: I miss my mattress topper." She points the slab at the park outside her window. "Caption: That dog just shit on the sidewalk." Then she plops out a breast and says, "Caption: Does this look like a lump to you?"

And there's the eight-year-old, who is the most comfortable being in a room with the slab. He's having the time of his life. He watches cartoons with the thing, has it read him stories, tell him jokes, show him pictures of naked ladies. He names it Mom. "Mom, you're my best friend," he tells it, and the slab thanks him. The final subject just lies in her bunk with her face to the wall, crying.

We explain all this to the men in lab coats at the end of each day. "Signs of cabin fever?" they ask. "Loneliness? Psychological hardship? Difficulties in device navigation?"

For the crier, sure, all the above. But each night the lab coats revise the software based on the day's failed commands and push out an update. This overjoys the subjects, that they can now do things that didn't work before.

The lab coats have us look through a printout of commands from the subjects' slabs, to see if there's anything the devices misunderstood.

The sheet says, among other things, Show me guys with no shirts. Click send. Dictate message to Matt Guy from Finnegan's. Click friends list. Send WhatsApp to Tim saying you better not be with Lisa. Hide this post from Dad. Look up popular gifts for sixty-two-year-old mothers of three. Tell me, why does it feel so good to let glue dry on your hand and peel it off? Send a message to Steve, The lady next door won't stop crying ha ha. Message to Derek, It was lonely here at first but not anymore, not with this thing they gave me. Tell me, is there intelligent life in the universe? Show me pictures of cute cats. Are any of them still alive? Download this pic from Insta and put me in it. Send sandwiches to my kids for dinner. Tell me a joke. Tell me a story. Tell me why Tamara from school doesn't like me. Vibrate. Vibrate harder. Don't stop vibrating, goddamnit. Tell me, Will I ever find love? Is Brad happy now, away from me? Tell me, How did Darwin form his theory? When will the sun cool? Where in the world are leaves reddest in autumn?

Jenna and I start sleeping together, doing our best to stave off boredom. Her slab shows us some lurid videos, and we try some things we see. But when cabin fever starts to bite at us both, we bite at each other in turn. She tells me I have a fat ass. I tell her she should learn to shiver better in bed. By the tenth day we barely speak, except to the slabs. When we happen upon a command they cannot perform—which is rare, increasingly rare—we decide it must not have been that important anyway.

Nine Point Five

MOM AND I SAT MUTE at the kitchen table, staring down at the poker cards in our hands while Dad and Jim yelled at each other on the front porch. We could hear them through the screen door. Though a fight between them was nothing new—they were friends from back before I was born—the sincerity of the anger in their voices was, and so were the personal accusations they leveled, referencing loyalty and courage and responsibility. The rubber factory where they worked was on strike and Jim had come over to tell my father he was crossing the picket line. He was trying to explain: He had two kids in college, a mortgage, car payments, all the rest. He couldn't live off the scraps the union provided. He had to think about his kids.

You want to talk to me about bills? Dad said.

What was also new was the way my father must have looked to Jim. I'd watched him shrink down over the last three months since the diagnosis, skin hanging loose around his face and neck like bunched-up cloth, his skin yellowed, his face and scalp and even eyelids bald.

Now was a hard time for us to be without Dad's salary, and Jim knew it. The union gave us a check each month in compensation, but it was a fraction of what the plant paid. Mom and I hadn't had any luck finding work ourselves, and no one was going to hire Dad with him looking the way he did. Then there was the issue of insurance, which Dad would lose if the strike went on much longer. He could buy coverage through COBRA, but that was hundreds of dollars more a month.

Jim tried again. He started to talk about stock prices and shipping costs and mechanized production and overseas distribution deals. Everybody knew the plant was doomed, he said, look at how many workers they'd laid off already. The union was holding on to something that wasn't there anymore.

I'm not a scab, Dad said.

Damn it, Daryl, you can call yourself whatever you want, Jim said. All you've got to do is cross the line, work a week or two, then file for medical disability. Now's not the time to play martyr.

At the kitchen table my mom asked for two new cards, not wanting to enter into the argument herself, not even wanting to overhear it. I dealt her what she asked for, marveling at the game's simplicity, where if you didn't like your cards you just asked for new ones.

When Dad first got the job, the plant must have seemed like something invincible. All the strengths of capitalism embodied in a huge, squat building smelling of hot rubber. Forklifts stacked crates impossibly high, machines molded and tested the belts and hoses, tires with varying treads lined the walkways. It was a place where the human beings, the small dots flitting between the piles of rubber goods, were not the main movers. They were part of something greater.

He wasn't looking for a factory job, though. After ten years of watching the small, family-owned farm dragged to the brink of extinction, he and Mom had sold theirs in time to make a little money and move to Lincoln, where he was studying to be a vet tech. Their budget was tight and he hated the science textbooks he had to study, but damn if he wouldn't be good in two years when he got the degree, if they could just hold on that long. He'd lived and worked with animals his whole life, milking them and feeding them and delivering their babies. He'd learned their anatomies not from books but from the precise curve of the butcher knives he'd used to carve out their meat for his family. He must have found it deeply satisfying, perched at the edge of fatherhood, to trade that butcher knife for a scalpel.

When the call came inviting him to interview at the factory, he thought it was a wrong number. Who are you trying to reach? he asked. The woman on the other end, not bothering to hide her annoyance, repeated his name back to him.

We got the number from your parents, she said. They told us you moved.

Dad stayed silent a moment, thinking back to before they'd sold the farm, vaguely remembering a job application he'd driven to the post office in his old Ford. He'd put his folks' number down because he knew his would be changing soon.

We've got a long application list, the woman said. Are you still interested in the position?

He looked at my mother across the table, my tiny feet kicking at the inside wall of her belly. They were living off what little money remained from the farm sale. His pride wouldn't allow them to accept state assistance, even though they qualified.

A steady paycheck, he must have thought. Not two years from now but now.

All right, he said. Yeah. I'm still interested.

Dad continued to work at the plant right up to the start of the strike, thirty-two hours a week because that's all he could fit in around his chemo schedule. Though I never told him, I was glad when the strike began. It meant he didn't spend those hours withering away in the plant with stiff muscles and bones, excusing himself (as I knew he must have) every so often to go puke in the plant toilet, a mess he'd probably clean up with crumpled toilet paper himself because he didn't want anyone else to have to. His whole life Dad had thought of providing for his family as a simple matter of keeping his head down and his mouth shut, so by the time he admitted to Mom and his doctor that something was wrong, that he was in pain, it had been too late to operate.

We didn't hear from Jim for several weeks after their fight. We survived on what little the union sent us. Sometimes we went to the union hall for our meals, where people from other unions dropped off casseroles and lasagnas to show their support. We ate off paper plates and left as soon as the men started to talk politics. The union leaned left and everyone liked to talk about what was wrong with America, the things that needed to change, and Dad wouldn't hear of it. Sometimes someone would ask him if he still talked to Jim, and he'd just shake his head.

Then came the roses. A dozen white ones, bundled up and placed in a pretty blue vase left on our doorstep.

What kind of man sends another man flowers? Dad asked when he read the tag, and left them sitting there on the porch.

I thought that would be the end of it, until a few days later Jim turned up on our doorstep himself. It was afternoon and I'd just gotten home from school. Mom and Dad were at chemo. The doorbell rang and I opened the door and there he was with a bottle of Johnnie Walker, a red bow fastened to its neck. As if to match he was wearing a red tie of his own for what must have been the first time in a long time, a thing so faded it looked pink.

Your dad home? he asked gruffly, eyes cast over my shoulder into the house, squinting into the bright winter light that filled it.

I shook my head. They're at the clinic.

Oh, he said. He looked down at the bottle he held, his ungloved hands clenched against the cold glass. He held it out to me. Can you give this to him, then?

I can if you want, but he can't drink whiskey anymore. It binds him up too much.

Ah hell. What about your mom?

Doesn't drink.

Jim looked down again at the label, brow knitted as if searching for some hint of possible action, then looked past me again through the doorway. Against the backdrop of his broad figure, the bottle looked practically toy-sized. He lowered his voice.

You'd tell me if your dad was home, now, wouldn't you?

Yeah, I'd tell you.

He picked nervously at the corner of the label with his thumbnail. I asked him if he'd like to come in.

Pretty soon we were at the table on the back patio, sipping scotch even though it was only half past three. He knew Dad let me drink sometimes when we had company, and anyway he'd added enough water to mine that it was several shades lighter. I watched him ash a cigarette on the mound of snow that filled the ashtray.

Daryl says you want to be a writer, he said.

Yeah, something like that.

What do you want to write?

I don't know. Books, I guess.

He took a long drag of his cigarette, trying to decode my answer. This was a man who dealt with physical products, things with tangible uses. Car tires, conveyor belts, rubber molded to whatever shape the bosses deemed fit. I might as well have told him I wanted to sell pixie dust for a living.

Your dad's some piece of work, you know. Stubborn as all hell.

I watched him crack his knuckles nervously, cigarette balanced in the corner of his lip.

All he's got to do is cross the line, work a few days, and file medical disability. Then he's got a steady paycheck and health insurance, and he doesn't even have to work for the plant. I know your dad. He won't be happy leaving you and Diane with nothing.

I know him too, I said. Well enough to know he's not going anywhere.

His face softened, like he'd just remembered something. Hey, of course. I'm talking long term here, twenty years from now. So he'll have something left when he's good and ready to retire.

I drained my glass and looked out into the yard. It was small but well-kept, snow unmussed and smooth on the ground, pine trees overhead neatly trimmed. Jim's comment had spoiled its peace.

I think you better get out of here, I said. Before Mom and Dad get home.

Sure, Jim said. Just let me finish my smoke.

On the way out he insisted on washing his glass with soapy water and setting it to dry in the rack by the sink, even though there was a dishwasher. Then he took mine and did the same, looking around the small kitchen. It wasn't much. A couple cabinets hung open, displaying their meager contents. Stacked cans of Walmart brand soup and beans, some ramen noodles, plain-looking bags of generic pasta. He drummed his fingers on the counter.

He turned back to me. You like whiskey, huh?

It's all right.

Well, I got a whole cabinet full of liquor and no one to drink it with. Your parents got chemo same time next week? Maybe I'll stop back by again.

It's a free country, I said, and led him to the door. After he left I sat at the kitchen table and poured myself another glass, no water this time, hands trembling with the feeling that the whole white snowy world was about to swallow up our little family.

When Jim showed up a week later, it was with two paper sacks of groceries. Standing out on the front porch, breath fogging in the cold, he told me they were filled mostly with canned goods and boxed meals. A little pickled herring, because he knew it was my father's favorite. Nothing fancy, he said. Nothing Diane will have to fuss over.

No way, I said. Dad will kill me.

I tried to shut the door but Jim stuck his boot between it and the jamb.

Hold on, he said, just listen a minute. I'm not taking this stuff back. So you got to either throw it in the trash and it all goes to waste, or help me take it inside and you and your family have some free food. You don't have to say it came from me.

I stood there a moment with my hand on the door, trying my best to glare him off the porch, but he wouldn't budge. So finally I said all right, fine, just get in here before the neighbors see. Together we unpacked the sacks, and when we finished we sat at the kitchen table and shared a drink.

From then on Jim came by with groceries each week. I told Mom and Dad that kids at school had taken up a donation for us, which Dad grumbled about but didn't refuse. Fresh salads in a bag, gallons of milk, hot dogs, sliced meat, hamburger helper, canned chicken, canned chili, sauce for sloppy joes, even charcoal and lighter fluid for the grill. Normally I think they would have gotten all sorts of donations like these. Friends coming by with casseroles and pies, tins of lasagna, etc. But most of their friends were either workers at the rubber factory or the wives of those workers. All on strike except Jim. Times were tight all around.

By the time Christmas neared, we had all agreed not to buy presents. The idea of our insurance premium quadrupling was seeming less and less like a threat and more and more like an eventuality. Dad had spent his whole life minding every dollar, so the idea of dipping into what we had saved for my college to pay our monthly expenses didn't sit well with him. He was intent on pinching what pennies we could, and that meant no presents.

Mom did what she could to look for work. But she hadn't had a job in a long time, and was finding it hard to break back into things—and hard, I suspect, to leave Dad at home alone. Still she looked half-heartedly in the Classifieds section every day for an opening for a housekeeper or a line cook or anything janitorial, anything where she didn't need to know how to use a computer. She knew how slow she typed. But she got so nervous for the interviews that every time she had one she pitted her shirts before she even left the house, a nervousness that couldn't have played well in the interviews.

I was writing these short pieces back then—I wouldn't even call them stories. I'd be walking to school and some detail would grab me, a dog sticking his snout out at me between the blinds of a neighbor's window or the way some pale green weeds poked through a crack in the sidewalk. I'd write these things down in a pocket-sized spiral notebook I kept under my bed and stare at them, trying to decipher what they meant to me. This notebook is the closest thing I have to a diary of this time, these pieces containing nothing about anything going on in my family, and in a way that silence says all there is to say.

Christmas came and went, small and sad. Jim hadn't been by with groceries for a couple weeks because he had family in town for the holidays. When he finally did come he said he wasn't feeling too well in the gut, he wasn't sure he could take any whiskey. I quietly suspected he'd begun to feel guilty for supplying me liquor, diluted though it always was. I got a couple off-brand colas from the cabinet and poured them over ice and sat down at the kitchen table. I began to describe Dad's latest doctor visits. I didn't look up at him. My eyes ached, and the words had a velvety feel coming out of my mouth.

His belly's getting bigger, I said. He looks like he's nine months pregnant with this thing. I went to the doctor with him last time and saw him with his shirt off, lying on his back on the table while the doctor felt around on him. His arms and neck are skinny as an old man's. And his liver isn't filtering fluids right, so his legs are so swollen it hurts to walk.

The doctors know what they're doing, Jim said. They're doing the best they can.

It's not just the pains, though, I said. He dozes off mid-sentence now. Sometimes he forgets who he's talking to, or he'll get confused by the simplest things we tell him.

It was here that we heard the automatic garage door rumble through the walls, the creak of it being hauled up the steel tracks Dad had said a long time ago he intended to oil, back before problems like a creaking door began to seem trivial.

We knew from that rumble we were caught. Jim made some frantic, futile attempts to get out the front door before they came in. He pulled on his work boots and fumbled at the laces until they were tied. He pulled on his coat from the back of his chair. Then he grabbed his glass of Coke and stood up, I guess meaning to run to the kitchen and throw it in the sink so Mom and Dad wouldn't think twice about why there were two glasses on the table instead of one. But by the time he got to his feet Mom and Dad were walking in from the garage, Dad's arm looped through my mom's as though he were being steadied in every step, a reversal of the way they used to walk. I watched Dad's eyes sweep the room, see Jim, see me, see the groceries on the table, comprehension widening then narrowing his glossy eyes.

Dad's voice had grown hoarse and ragged, more so than I had realized, but that did not stop him from raising it at Jim. It was the first time I'd heard him yell at his friend where Jim did not raise his voice in turn. There was a horrifying sort of humor to the scene—my dad looked positively alien standing there with swollen legs and a swollen gut, head and face completely bald but for a few straggly gray hairs, screaming in a ragged voice that he did not need Jim's help. Jim glanced at me and I looked away, to my mother, then my eyes followed hers to the floor.

When Dad was done, I stood up and walked Jim to the door. I didn't look at Dad but saw him slumped in the periphery, chest heaving. I let Jim out and said I was sorry, a sentiment that seems laughably insufficient to me now, though I still don't know what I would rather have said.

Dad went into the bedroom to lie down. I went to the kitchen to help Mom unpack the groceries. Together we stacked soup cans in the cupboard, threw out the old spoiled vegetables from the crisper to make room for the new, and set some frozen drumsticks running under cold water in the sink to thaw for dinner.

It's not fair, I said quietly. The way he's treating Jim.

Mom kept unpacking and said that wasn't our call to make. In a flat voice she told me the reason she and Dad were home early from treatment was that Dr. Berg said the chemo was no longer working. They needed to try a new mix of drugs. I asked her if they thought that would work. If she thought that would work. She said she didn't know.

On New Year's Eve I took some steaks out of the deep freeze in the garage, steaks we'd been saving, and a salmon fillet for Dad. He could no longer eat beef, but he insisted that Mom and I did.

I sat in the corner of the living room with a collection of short stories I was rereading distractedly, underlining lines I liked, marking up the margins, looking at Dad every time he shifted positions with a pained look on his face. He was reclined in his chair, eyes shut, Fox News on the TV turned down to a low murmur to lull him to sleep. Mom flipped through the Classifieds section. She hummed something tuneless to herself and stared at the screen and every so often glanced over at her husband.

In the early evening Dad's sleep got more restless. He shifted side to side, hands on his belly. Eventually his eyes opened and he asked for more pills. I ran and got them, willing my heart not to pound so loud. He slept another fitful thirty minutes, then stood up. He began to pace, hand on his lower back, swollen legs plodding heavily. Eventually he turned to me and said, I think you'd better start the car.

The world was bright white. Snow piled in drifts on either side of the road, cars so covered they looked like giant mounds of snow. Slick ice underfoot and under the wheels. I drove because my eyesight was best. Dad sat in the front seat, leaned way back, eyes closed. Mom was in the back middle seat, leaned forward so she could keep her eyes on Dad. The wipers batted furiously at the snow. Frost and fog crept in from the corners of all the windows, gradually shrinking my visible field.

Racing down 56th Street toward O, maybe a mile from the emergency room, a light turned red and I floored the brake pedal. Nothing happened. I felt the brakes kick underfoot, skipping across the surface of the ice like a flat stone on a body of water. We just kept barreling toward the intersection, one of the busiest there was in town, blurred headlights crisscrossing our path. I had enough time to glance over at Dad and see he was asleep, then I jerked the steering wheel sharply to the right and jumped the curb into a parking lot. The brakes caught traction. We skidded to a stop. I got out of the car and heard the hiss of air escaping tires.

I stood outside with Mom, flakes of snow swirling against our hair and faces. Dad was still reclined in the front seat, looking out at us, trying to hide his discomfort. Is it bad? he asked.

A couple of flats, I said. I breathed warm air into my cupped hands, trying to regain feeling. The hospital was still a mile away, and there was no way Dad could walk.

We'll never get a cab, I said. I think we need to call 9-1-1.

Dad looked at the dash, chewing the inside of his cheek. Do you have your phone? he asked my mother.

She nodded yes.

Son of a bitch. Give it here.

She handed it to him through the open window. I watched him flip it open and punch in a number from muscle memory.

When Jim arrived the snow had stopped. We were sitting in the car with the heat on full blast, waiting, and we all piled into his pickup. Were you at home? Dad asked. Jim said no, he was at work. He'd told the supervisor Daryl needed his help and they'd let him go with no questions.

In the emergency room, the doctor hooked Dad up to an IV and felt around on his belly. He gave Dad a button to squeeze if he needed more morphine. He was amazed at the size of the liver. They were trying to reach Dr. Berg, who had the day off. He looked at the notes my mom had of the medications my dad was on, the doses and the time he had to wait between the doses. The medicines he was to take as needed. He asked Dad to rate his pain.

Nine, he said. Maybe nine point five. He squeezed the button.

Dad detailed his medicinal routine for the doctor. He explained how the pain had been getting steadily worse. He said that each day he hurt a little more, tried to distract himself with the newspaper or the TV and just, you know, tough it out. This was all news to me. I knew he was hurting, but not how serious the pain had gotten. Dad usually talked about it the way you'd talk about a mild headache, some minor irritation. I listened as he told the doctor he didn't like to take the pills deemed "as needed."

I wouldn't say I *need* them, he explained, pressing the button in his hand absently. The doctor asked him if Dr. Berg knew these things he was saying and he said no.

The doctor was sitting in a chair beside the bed. He put his clipboard down. He looked around at the rest of us. An alarm sounded nearby, and there was the frantic shuffle of nurses' feet in front of our door. The doctor had on his face a mixture of confusion and impatience. He looked back to my dad. You have cancer, he said. You're going to be in pain. What we can do for you is we can give you medicine, then you take that medicine, and if you need more you tell us you need more.

He stood up. We'll tell you when we talk to Dr. Berg. He will prescribe you new, stronger medication.

After he left Dad shut his eyes and they began to tremble beneath the lids. I could tell from how tight his lips were pursed that he wasn't asleep. I could see the trepidation there, the embarrassment, the fear. And I knew that in his position I wouldn't have said anything about the pain either. That I had that piece of him in me, the piece that would rather let the pain eat at me than grant it the power of a name.

Mom and I stood outside in the hall, sipping coffee from Styrofoam cups. We watched the nurses walk by in blue scrubs. A man with one leg balanced on a crutch to fish money from his pocket for a fruit juice. Jim was in the room with my dad. They'd asked for a moment alone.

Mom and I made small talk. I blew on my cup of coffee, watching the black liquid ripple, the steam rise. Every little bit seemed significant now: the bright lights, the man with one leg, the sign on the juice machine indicating they were out of orange. I was drowning in the details. Mom asked me about school, if I'd kept up with my homework. Her questions dazed me. I couldn't remember the last time we'd talked about something that wasn't Dad.

I interrupted her. This is bad, right? I said. This new pain?

She looked away, blowing carefully at the surface of her own coffee. A small, simple task she could easily understand. I nodded gently to myself, as though she'd said something profound.

Down the hall, a fluorescent light flickered above Dad's cracked door. Through the crack I saw Dad's foot at the end of the bed, shifting listlessly under the white sheet. I wanted desperately to be in there with him, to hear what he and Jim were saying. To be able to say here now what he said to Jim in that room. But this isn't my story. I am in the hallway, trying to peer in.

A week before Dad died, the strike ended and the plant reopened at reduced capacity. The workers with a lot of years under their belts got better benefits, better pay. Their jobs were protected. But the new hires, the next generation, had none of this. They made barely better than fast food money. And a few years later, when the plant was sold for a pittance to some foreign company, the few senior workers who stayed on were reduced to this low wage as well.

Dad was barely aware it was over. After the trip to the emergency room, we didn't read the paper or turn on the news. Maybe we let a compact disc spin in the corner, a crisp digital sound. Maybe we left the TV on, tuned to the nature channel or something soothing like that. For a few more weeks we tried chemo. Then they told us it wasn't working and sent us home with a prescription for liquid morphine to make him more comfortable. Dad ate less and less and slept more and more. One day he woke up long enough for us to tell him we loved him, then he stopped breathing.

We later learned that five weeks before his death, Dad's life insurance policy was up for renewal, with the option to double down on the amount. He had happily signed. He must have been aware that this renewal was looming, if he could just hold on that long. It was a surprise going away present we found out about when a nice letter came in the mail from the insurance company. It said they were sorry for our loss. So now Mom could take her time finding a job, if she even wanted one. The money for my college was in the bank. We were touched and elated and furious, baffled by what we had gained and lost.

A decade later, I ran into Jim in the Denver airport on my way to a conference. We were both coming from different parts of the country, there for a quick layover, just passing through on our way somewhere else. I offered to buy him a glass of Johnnie Walker and he said sure, he didn't drink much anymore but what the hell.

We sat in a cramped back booth of a brightly lit airport restaurant, fluorescent lights garish as a hospital room. After half a drink I leaned the side of my head lightly against the big bay window and looked out onto the runway at all the passing planes. Jim said he'd recently quit smoking again and I said congratulations.

I still think about your old man, he told me. About them last couple months.

I nodded absently. I do too, I said. Though some of it's getting fuzzy.

He said he was sure I'd remember what was important.

I drained my last bit of scotch, grimacing. I'd never had the heart to tell Jim I didn't much care for the stuff. I'd invited him to a drink because I wanted to ask him what they talked about in the hospital room that night, but I'd lost my nerve. Suddenly I felt like that scared teenager again, and I didn't know if I could get the words out without my voice breaking. At a certain point, I thought, it must be better to let a wound heal poorly then to open it back up again. So I slid my empty glass to the center of the table and told him I had a flight to catch.

We stood up and shook hands. Jim said he had one last question, if

I didn't mind. Anything, I said. He asked what we did with the ashes, since we hadn't had plans yet at the funeral. I told him we scattered them on the first day of spring, at the farm where I was conceived. He nodded approvingly. I wish I knew him back then, he said. Before the rubber factory.

At the gate I wheeled my suitcase to an empty seat on the row facing the runway. I glanced up at the screen above the airline counter and saw the flight had been delayed. I wanted to get some reading done—because somewhere along the way that's what reading had become for me, a thing that needed to be "got done"—but I didn't have the energy. Instead I sat and watched the other people at the gate. Men and women in suits squinting at their laptop screens. Children with boxes of crayons going at coloring books with all their might. The woman at the counter leaning into the microphone to make her crackly voice better heard. Outside planes zoomed in for a landing or heaved themselves up into the air, impossibly heavy metal heaps made to fly, while inside air traffic controllers tabulated the data.

What That Meant in Miles

MIDGE STUMBLED A BIT, and almost fell forward onto the footholds the guide had stamped in the ice. Sixty-six years old, she was already fatigued, not even a third of the way up. Each step toward the volcano's summit deepened the dull but persistent pain in her calves, and every breath of cold air ripped at the inside of her lungs. She regained her footing, paused, and looked toward the bottom of the steep slope. The idea of tumbling down that white, frictionless sheet made her palms sweat, at the same time she was invigorated to see how far they had come.

Her husband, Henry, was several steps ahead and hadn't seen her stumble. But the Russian hiker behind her cleared his throat. "Are you all right?" he asked.

She was startled by how confident his English sounded. "Yes, I'm fine. I was just taking it all in."

At the front of the group, the head guide, Felipe, fashioned their path. For each step, he formed a foothold by slicing his pickaxe down into the ice and kicking the incision. Behind him, Henry watched in admiration, imagining Felipe's life as best he could. He asked the man in Spanish how often he made this ascent and he said cuatro veces por semana. Imagine that! Four times a week up the face of an active volcano. Waking before dawn, at the summit by noon, then back down and having a drink before sunset. A hell of a life to lead. Henry would never tire of a life like that.

There were nine of them in all, trekking single file in a zigzag pattern up the slope: Felipe, a younger guide whose name Henry didn't know, him and Midge, the Russian, and four Swiss girls. Henry had meant to be farther back, with Midge, but in his eagerness had fallen in line right behind Felipe. Before they began, Henry had tried out what German he knew on the Swiss and had done all right, he thought, until they started talking back. Midge had been on him lately to get a hearing aid, but he'd dismissed this advice.

Henry was keeping up with Felipe just fine, though the vibrations from the pickaxe were starting to bother his hand. He held it like the guide had said, driving the spike down into the ice with each step, always on higher ground so if he fell he could hang on to it rather than be impaled. Deaths on the volcano were rare, but not impossible. There was nothing to grab on to once you started rolling down, no way to stop the terrible inertia.

He wanted to pause for a moment, to squeeze his hand into a fist. This sometimes helped the arthritis, to let a little air into the joints. But he didn't want to hold up the others, and it was too soon to start taking breaks just yet.

Midge's breathless spell had passed quickly. Her throat was dry and the small of her back ached, but her feet fell steadily again. No more stumbles. After a while the guides let them stop on a flat space next to three gray boulders sticking out of the snow. They were told in English to sit down. Midge took off her sunglasses and looked out onto the landscape. The sky was brighter blue than anything she'd ever seen, and all the surrounding mountains, their solid masses straining up into the sky, seemed intent on reminding her how much longer they'd be around than she would.

Henry sat down beside her on one of the boulders. "My god," he said. "That Russian has no sleeves."

"Shh. He speaks English."

"It can't be more than twenty degrees out here. Where are the boy's sleeves?"

"I'm sure he's used to the cold."

"What is that in Celsius, anyway? Twenty degrees."

Midge tried to calculate. "Ten below, maybe? I don't know. Give me some water."

Henry took the bottle out of his pack. "Here. You better have a cereal bar too, if you're half as hungry as I am."

"A cup of coffee, that's what I could use. Why didn't we bring the thermos?"

"You must have forgotten to volunteer to carry it," Henry said, and winked.

Felipe clambered up the tallest boulder. Cupping his hands dramatically around his mouth, he called out that in five more minutes they'd move on.

"He can't be serious," Midge said. "We just sat down."

Her face was covered in sweat and she shivered when the cold wind hit it.

"Try not to think about it," Henry said. "Here, let me get your coat."

Henry leaned over and dug in her backpack for the puffy jacket the tour company had provided. She put out her arms and he helped her get it on. "Funny how you don't notice the cold when you're moving," he said. Before they'd been fine in just sweatshirts.

"How's your arthritis?" she asked.

"Hush," he said. "You don't want these people knowing I'm an old man, do you?" He kissed her on the cheek. "I'm going to go ask the guide a question. I feel like speaking Spanish."

Midge smiled and shivered and looked out at the view. The way the clouds jutted up against the white snowy summits made it look like pieces of the taller mountains were floating away, becoming clouds.

The air here was a hell of a thing. It was thin and cold and pure. She felt like it could cure anything. Like she could bring a jar of it back to the US and tell someone who was feeling sad, "Here, just take a deep breath of this." Poof! Their depression would disappear. Midge knew this was silly but still half believed it. At first she'd been reluctant to attempt this climb, but now was sure it was just the type of thing they'd been missing for so many years. For a long time they'd been saving every penny so they could travel the world when they retired. This three-week trip through Chile was just the start. And why not? They had nothing tying them to any one place.

The Russian came and sat down beside her. He still hadn't put on his jacket. He introduced himself as Vlad.

"Midge," she said. "Aren't you cold?"

"We will be moving again soon. How are you feeling?"

Her cheeks suddenly grew warm. "I'm fine," she said. "I think I just needed water."

"You are very strong. I hope I am climbing volcanoes when I am your age. You have children?"

Midge looked down at her feet, as if she were studying the way the laces lay on her boots. She felt a familiar pressure, as if her rib cage were suddenly pressing in on her heart and lungs. This was not a conversation she wanted to have. But after all these years she still didn't know the graceful way to avoid it. *I used to have a son* is not a thing people let slide by without questions and condolences. So she said what she always said.

"No. I don't have children."

• • •

As they trotted up the great white slope, it filled with other trekking parties. Most were bigger than their own, and many moved faster. Each group had its own color jacket. Midge and Henry's were sky blue, the color of baby clothes.

Henry was disappointed their group had no Chileans. Four Swiss and a Russian, that was no good. "Dónde están los chilenos?" he asked Felipe.

Felipe motioned gruffly toward a cluster of hikers in red jackets, and responded in English. "If they are here, they are in the big groups, not the small ones. Cheaper that way."

Behind them, Midge listened and started to feel dizzy. Her throat was suddenly dry and her head hurt again. She concentrated on setting one foot in front of the other, pickaxe point pressed firmly into the ice.

Henry tried again to get Felipe to speak Spanish with him. "Ustedes tienen un país hermoso."

Again Midge stumbled, worse this time. Her boot overshot the foothold and skidded rightward, down the slope. She let out a cry. Clinging tight to the cold pickaxe handle, she tried to regain her balance, but her other knee began to buckle. From behind, two large, gentle hands steadied her under her armpits. She squeezed her arms tight to her sides and it was like when she was a child, a thermometer under her arm, her mother telling her *Keep it tight against your body*. She felt unbearably light, like whoever was holding her could just swaddle her and carry her easily to the summit.

"Careful," Vlad said in her ear. "You feel sick?"

Midge nodded. She shook the Russian off and sat down in the snow, suddenly surrounded by concerned faces. She took off her sunglasses, but it was too bright so she put them back on. Then Henry was crouching on the snow beside her, asking what was wrong, was something wrong?

"I think she's dizzy," Vlad said. "She almost fell."

She looked up at the Russian and he was the age of her son, the age her son was, when.

"We should go back down," Henry said.

"No. I'll be fine."

"Baby, we're not even halfway up."

She smiled. She loved this about him, that after all these years he still called her baby.

"I'll be fine. I have some aspirin in my backpack."

Though she was sitting in snow, she couldn't feel the cold through the snow pants they'd given her. Henry dug in her backpack for the aspirin. He handed it to her, along with some water to take it with.

"You need to drink a lot of water," Felipe said. "For the sickness."

"Will she be all right?"

"She will be fine. But maybe she should try to climb another day."

"There is no other day. Tomorrow we're off to Punta Arenas, then Torres del Paine."

"It can be dangerous if she is dizzy. And we are losing time."

Henry looked around the slope. There were still groups below them, but fewer than before. They were being overtaken. The younger guide said something to Felipe and gestured toward the peak.

Henry looked down at his hand and squeezed it into a fist, trying to loosen the joints. This had been his damn fool idea, this climb. Midge had said it might be too much for them, but he'd refused to believe it. It was the sort of thing they'd put off for so long. A lifetime, it seemed. And now the time had passed. What was he doing here, crouched on the side of a volcano with aching knuckles and a poor wife he'd made sick by being so stubborn?

She took his hand. "You go on ahead. One of the guides can take me back down."

"Like hell."

"It's okay. Really. I'm just as happy to wait at the hotel."

Henry stood up. "And then what? I go for another half hour then get dizzy too and go down by myself? No, you were right. We shouldn't have come."

He looked up at the sky. Two distant mountains cradled the sun, as good a view as he was going to get. He took the camera out of his jacket's breast pocket, snapped a picture, and turned to the younger guide. "Puede bajar con nosotros?"

The guide nodded yes, he could take them down.

"Listen to me, will you?" Midge said. "I want you to keep going."

He put the camera back in his pocket. He sat down beside her and put his head on her shoulder. Her jacket was big and bulky and soft on his cheek. "No, I don't want to. It's no good without you. If we can't go up together we can at least go down together."

She looked around at the other travelers. The Russian had put on a coat. The Swiss girls were standing with their arms crossed, speaking German to one another in low tones. One glanced at her then looked away with an expression like she'd just sniffed sour milk. They wanted to get moving again. Part of Midge wanted to go with them. A large part. A part she forced herself to ignore.

For some minutes the guides spoke to each other in machine-gun Spanish too fast to follow. They seemed to be arguing. The younger guide kept pointing up to the peak and Felipe was shaking his head no. Felipe said something into his walkie-talkie and listened to the crackly response. He nodded, his eyes on the younger guide. "Vale," he said. Then he addressed the tour group: "I'm afraid we cannot take Midge back down, not yet."

He explained that their boss was very strict, and that climbing higher with the rest of them would mean too many hikers to a single guide. Instead, Felipe would continue on with the Swiss while the other guide, Pato, stayed behind with Henry and Midge and Vlad. That group would move slower up the mountain, with more breaks, so another guide could catch up with them. Then if Midge and Henry still needed to go down they could.

Midge felt bad for Vlad, for making him hang back. She told him so.

Vlad shook his head. "Altitude sickness is common. It can happen to anyone."

"It didn't, though," she said. "It happened to me."

. . .

When they started up again, Midge walked up front, behind Pato. She watched his slow, methodical work with the pickaxe. After a while he stopped, turned his head slightly, and called back over his shoulder. "Everyone okay?"

She didn't like that. She knew it was a question for her, and she knew Henry and Vlad knew it too.

"I'm fine," she called back. "Thank you." When he started walking again and she was sure no one would see, she stuck her tongue out at him.

When Henry had first brought it up, Midge had been nervous about the climb, sure it would make them feel their age. She had pictured her and Henry trailing behind a bunch of twenty-something body-building backpackers who would barely break a sweat. But by the time they'd arrived in Chile, the volcano had transformed in her mind into something of pure beauty, a once-in-a-lifetime opportunity. The night before the climb, this had excited her to no end. She had been outright giddy, and she and Henry made love for the first time in ages. She laughed as he fumbled with the childproof cap on the prescription pill bottle. "Here," she said, "let me." He turned red. "At least we don't have to use condoms, right?" she said. He smiled and nodded and kissed her deeply. But when he pushed her back on the bed and started to undo her belt, fingers growing surer, she looked up at the chain dangling from the ceiling fan and felt strange remembering how long they had used condoms after they were first married, how excited they were when they stopped so they could start trying for Billy. When they finished she was sure he saw the tears in the corners of her eyes.

She heard Henry behind her now, and knew he was hurting. The pain in his hands. The pickaxe would be hard to hold. She'd lived with him living with his pains so long they felt like her own. His legs would be aching too, but he'd be too scared to say so. He wanted to be the strong one, to impress her and the guide and poor sweet Vlad, who'd had to stay behind with them. So let Henry be the rock. When they got back down he'd confess his hands and legs had been hurting, and she would say, *Oh! I had no idea.* This was the story of her life with Henry. His hidden pains, her bleeding out in the open despite all her best efforts.

They walked for some time with no break. Henry was in the back. He wanted to be watching Midge, to make sure she was all right, but he had to keep his eyes on where his feet were falling. He had to trust the guide, the Russian, the grips on Midge's shoes. He knew she'd stop if she needed to. She'd be embarrassed, but she would stop. And he knew that Vlad would catch her again if need be, and damn it if he wouldn't do a better job than Henry ever could. Anyway, it seemed her spell had passed.

Eventually they rested on a big rock and had lunch. They were now the only group on this part of the volcano; everyone else was farther up, and many would be at the top already. They made small talk while they waited for the other guide. Henry took Midge's hand. It was a strange sensation, holding someone else's gloved hand with his own, the material bunching between them. A touch without warmth, like resting a hand on the body in a casket.

After a while Pato took out his walkie-talkie and started talking. Something staticky answered back. "¿Cómo?" he said, again and again. "Sí, sí, OK, entiendo."

He put the walkie-talkie back in his bag.

"The other guide isn't coming," Midge said.

Henry looked from her to Pato. "Is that what they said?

"We do not have enough workers today," the guide said. "They have no one to send."

"So what do we do?"

"We keep moving. We hope your wife is okay. If no, we all go down together."

Before they started moving again, Midge went off with Pato to find a place for her to pee. As private a place as one could find on a wide-open slope above the tree line. The guide walked ahead of her, carving out steps in the snow until they found a flat spot half-hidden between some large rocks. He stood with his arms crossed and his back turned as she unbuckled and squatted, steam rising around her.

Meanwhile, Vlad and Henry shared an energy bar and an awkward silence. Henry felt unmanned by Vlad, who had kept his wife from falling.

"Your wife is a good woman," Vlad said. "How long have you been married?"

"Forty-one years."

The Russian whistled. "I cannot imagine knowing someone so well. All that time, just the two of you."

Henry licked his lips. "What do you mean?"

"Midge says to me you do not have children."

Henry trained his eyes on the interweaving sets of footprints leading up to them, unable to tell which were theirs.

"That's only half true," he told Vlad. He licked his lips again, flaps of dead skin chapped from the cold. This was the conversation he never wanted to have but always ended up having anyhow. He suddenly felt a bit lightheaded himself, and took a deep drink of water.

They had had a son once, Henry wanted to say, but that didn't seem like the type of thing one said. Not there, trapped with this man at who knew how many meters above sea level or what that number meant in miles anyway. A million little interventions he might have made, that was what Henry would always remember. Especially that answering machine tape, that last message Billy had left, and the cassette player that ate it: Henry with his clumsy arthritic fingers and bad vision made worse by tears, tugging desperately until the ribbon ripped. They'd never thought to make a copy, wouldn't have known how without Billy. One last failure to intervene, one last loss chalked up to bad luck. Just one of those things. Everything was always just one of those things.

When Billy was born he was blue-faced and not breathing, umbilical cord wrapped around his neck. Henry was stuck in an airport in Pennsylvania, traveling for business like usual, pacing back and forth. Something in the way the clouds hovered outside the bay windows told him it was all wrong. The first and only birth Henry had witnessed was as a child, a prolapsed heifer at his uncle's farm in Norfolk, her insides turning inside out as the calf was born. A bad omen. He was not religious nor superstitious but he wasn't blind either. They unwrapped the cord immediately but the boy was never quite right. Stole a car at sixteen just to show he could, abandoned it still running in an Osco parking lot. Sold the younger kids at his school spray paint to huff. They knew the drinking was a problem, and the driving too, but it was just one of those things.

But Henry didn't tell the Russian any of this. Instead he found himself telling him about the tape and the damn machine that ate it. Midge had been on him to get a new cassette player for the bedroom. It was as old as Billy was when the accident happened, the geometric symbols on the gray buttons all but smudged away. Some nights, when Midge could sleep and he couldn't, Henry would pop in the tape and watch the white spindles rotate. Here came Billy's voice, "Hey ma, it's Bill, just wanted to say, you know, thanks for everything..." It was from the night following the intervention, when after a lot of tears and fessing up and hand-wringing he'd sworn off the bottle. There was something in his voice on that recording that Henry couldn't stop going back to. It was shaky in all the right ways, filled with a worn, tired kind of perseverance Henry had never heard before.

"I remember thinking," Henry said, "that this is what hope sounds like. This is what I need to carry forward. But now for the life of me I can't hear it in my head. I can't remember my own son's voice. I remember hearing it, and what I thought at the time, but I can't hear the thing itself. Not now that the damn machine ate the tape."

Midge came crunching back across their boot prints from before. Over the rhythmic steps came Henry's voice. As she got closer she started to pick out some words and she understood what he was talking about. What, though maybe not why. Something about that tape, it tore at Henry. She'd tried so many times to tell him it was bound to happen. A cassette tape was not a permanent medium. Nothing was. But it didn't matter. He wouldn't hear her.

"Henry—"

She was standing next to the guide now, a few feet away from Henry and Vlad, who sat together on a small boulder. Vlad had an all-too-familiar look on his face, full of pity and deep discomfort. He glanced at her for a moment then quickly looked away.

Soon they were moving again. She didn't know what to say to Henry nor to Vlad, so she didn't say anything. They were all but alone on the slope now. The cold air bit at her lips and eyes and her whole was body sore, fatigued. Sweat pooled in her armpits and slicked the palms of her hands. The air grew thinner and thinner, her breath more ragged, the exertion more exhausting. She watched her steps fall, trying to block out all else. They had been walking for so long but she was certain if she stopped she would not start again. She started to feel dizzy and told herself, *No. This is not what happens here. The guide said we were close.*

Henry was behind her, wheezing. Ahead, the Russian, grunting. She beat back the urge to look up at the sky. She had to be careful where she put her feet. One wrong step and down you went. One wrong step was all it took. But her thoughts felt lighter up here in the thin air. Like lily pads floating down a stream. In her mind's eye she saw herself trip and fall sideways, losing her grip on the pickaxe, tumbling down the slick white surface. How many years would that cut her life short, anyway? Twenty, thirty? Maybe ten, or even less? They wouldn't call that a tragedy. Somewhere along the way she'd reached the age where death became unfortunate, rather than tragic.

She tried to let her mind clear, to let her senses carry her. She heard her husband wheezing behind her, Pato whistling up ahead. Her cold, ragged breath sliced into her like a handsaw, pressure building in her kneecaps until she was sure they would burst. How long had her knees been aching? Maybe forever.

Glancing down she could not tell where she was on the volcano. It seemed like the same stretch of footprints they'd been walking for hours. *We're going in circles*, she thought wildly. *They've tricked me. They've found a way to always move up but never reach the top.* Then she felt a strange, quaint certainty that if she turned around she would not see the gray-haired Henry who shared her bed last night and almost every night these last four decades, but the hippie with a long black beard who first winked at her at age twenty-one and offered her a drag off his cigarette. It was not an altogether unpleasant thought.

"Henry?"

He huffed along behind her.

"Yes, I'm here."

"I don't feel so well."

Henry looked up. He saw that he and Midge had fallen behind. The others were ahead by a couple dozen paces or more.

"Okay, Midge, stop there."

She slowed, but took another step.

"Midge, baby, it's okay. Wait where you are."

"Do your hands hurt?" she asked.

He squeezed his right hand into a fist. It felt like a small explosion of white-hot pinpricks between the joints.

"I guess they do," he said.

"It's strange how you don't notice the pain after a while. Unless someone brings it up."

She took another step.

"Midge, cut it out!" he said. He took hold of the back of her coat with his free hand. The other held fast to his pickaxe speared into the slope beside him. "Just stay still a minute," he said.

Midge turned and twisted her body back toward him the best she could without stepping outside her footprints.

"What's wrong?" she asked. She let her pickaxe go and grabbed onto his arm gently with both her hands.

"Here, sit down," he said.

"Did you know you look like Billy? I suppose you don't notice."

"Listen, I'm sorry I brought it up. Blame the altitude. No, blame the Russian."

"He's a good boy, you know."

"The Russian? I know. I'm just joking. Listen, sit down a minute."

"Not the Russian."

Henry's mind stuttered. "Who do you mean, honey? You mean Billy?"

Midge half fell, half sat down in the snow. She looked around, lost.

"Henry. Henry's a good boy."

Up ahead, Vlad and Pato had stopped. Henry couldn't see the expressions on their faces but Pato was pointing back at them. Henry held up a single finger. One second. Just wait one second.

"Who did you say? Who's a good boy?" He sat down beside her. He took her hand. If they could just bide their time. Wait for her to get her bearings before they tried to move.

"Henry. I know you don't like him. His hair is too long."

"Midge, who do you think I am?" he whispered.

Confusion crept across her face, written in the folds that formed as she narrowed her eyes. Her lips moved slightly, as if reading a set of complicated instructions. Still she clasped his hand. Henry's heart galloped along faster and faster as she studied him.

"¡Amigo!" he heard Pato call. "¿Todo bien?"

"¡Esperen!" Henry called back. "Wait one minute, damn it!"

He looked back at Midge. She wiggled her hand in his and giggled.

They'd seen this sort of thing in both their mothers, at the end. But this was too soon, just too soon. Sure, Midge could be spacy. They both could. He'd noticed her water the plants twice in one day, or unlock the front door when she thought she was locking it. Once she'd tried to make an appointment with the dentist and called their old dentist, from years prior and several states over. She hadn't realized her mistake until halfway through the conversation, then hung up the phone red as a beet without a word. They'd both eventually laughed at that, though, thought nothing of it. Now a million similar instances jumped to his mind, a tapestry he'd refused to see as a whole.

He looked into her eyes and tried not to see an icy glimmer of things to come. "It's just the altitude, Midge," he said. "You'll feel better in a minute."

She nodded. "I'm starting to feel better now."

He glanced up to where Pato and Vlad were standing, watching and waiting. Then, for the first time, he noticed that there was hardly any more mountain above them.

"My god," he said. "I think that's the top. Right over that ridge there." He called out to Pato, pointing. "Is that the peak?"

"¡Sí, claro!" the guide shouted back, hands cupped around his mouth. "We are almost there!"

Henry looked at Midge and she was looking back at him. She dug into her pack and pulled out a bottle of water. Smiled. And with that it was her, Midge was Midge again.

"Billy loved this about you," she said. "This stubbornness."

Henry wasn't sure what she meant. "Pato says that's it, right up there," he said.

She took a long gulp of water. "Remember when you bought Billy that Nintendo, then stayed up all night with his friends helping them beat Super Mario?"

Henry smiled. "We thought the damn thing was broken at first. We were sure it couldn't be so hard."

They fell silent. The sounds drifted down from the peak. They could hear the other tour groups now, whooping and hollering in several different languages.

"I think I'm ready," Midge said, and handed him the bottle of water.

Farther up the slope, Vlad watched Henry help Midge up. She seemed shaky. At first Vlad wished he'd noticed sooner that they were falling behind, and stayed down there with them. Then he was glad he hadn't.

Beside him, Pato muttered something that sounded like profanity. Vlad didn't understand Spanish. As he watched, Henry guided Midge's hand to the pickaxe she'd left standing in the snow, then grabbed his own pickaxe, holding on to the back of her jacket the whole time. Midge took a shaky step forward, then Henry took one too. After Midge took a second step, surer now, so did Henry.

"Chucha," Pato said to Vlad. "We will be here forever."

Vlad waved his hand dismissively. He took a flask out of his pocket, figuring they were past the hard part, and while he drank he decided to return to this volcano when he was Henry's age, to prove that he could still do it too. All around them, the wind whistled across the hardened snow.

Below, Henry and Midge wound their way up the volcano. Vlad and Pato watched the old couple in silence, and after a while it was impossible to tell who was helping who, Henry holding Midge aloft by the back of her coat or Midge guiding Henry forward, one wavering step at a time.

ACKNOWLEDGMENTS

I WANT TO THANK Margot Livesy, who selected this book for publication, and everyone at the University of Iowa Press who ushered it out into the world. I am also grateful to the editors who previously supported this work by publishing the following stories: "The Knack" in *Sycamore Review*, "In Case I Don't Call" in *Joyland*, "There, There" in *The Adroit Journal*, "The Brightmore Problem" in *Sequestrum*, "Snapshots" in *The Los Angeles Review*, "All the Wild" in *Midwestern Gothic*, "Breath" in *Wigleaf* and *Best Microfiction 2023*, "The So-Called Jacob" in *Quarter After Eight*, "Consider It Saved" in *Cutthroat*, "Now Nothing" in *Hypertext*, "The Slabs" in *The Cincinnati Review MiCRO Series*, "Sayings" in *The Able Muse*, "Nothing Is Ever So Simple as Zombies" in *decomP magazinE*, and "What That Meant in Miles" in *Prime Number Magazine*. In addition, many thanks to the Ecuadorian press Cactus Pink for publishing my chapbook *Snapshots*, which included the following stories along with Spanish translations: "The Knack," "There, There," "Snapshots," "The Slabs," and "Nothing Is Ever So Simple as Zombies."

Thank you to all the great writing teachers and fellow writers who gave me feedback on my work over the years—with a special shout-out to Aimee Bender, whose workshop was what inspired me to stretch beyond the realist mode. I'd also like to express my gratitude to the creative writing departments at the University of Nevada–Las Vegas and the University of Southern California, especially for their flexibility in letting me live abroad during the completion of my degrees.

Special thanks to Oscar and Ben, for their love and friendship and dedication to keeping my whiskey glass full. And to all the writers in Ecuador who so generously welcomed me into their community during my time there, especially Santiago Peña Bossano and the other authors at Cactus Pink.

Thank you to my father, who taught me the importance of doing good work with no pretension. My mother, who taught me not only to read but to be a reader. My brother, for turning me on to so much good art so young. And Kuzco and Kronk, whom I miss dearly, my companions while writing much of this book. There's no better way to stay alert than having a cat that bites you any time you go too long without petting it.

Above all, thank you to Brandy, for this perfect life that we have built, and to my children, Darwin and Juniper, who remind me every day that some joys are too big for words to hold.

THE IOWA SHORT FICTION AWARD AND THE JOHN SIMMONS SHORT FICTION AWARD WINNERS, 1970–2025

Lee Abbott
Wet Places at Noon
Cara Blue Adams
You Never Get It Back
Donald Anderson
Fire Road
Dianne Benedict
Shiny Objects
A. J. Bermudez
Stories No One Hopes Are about Them
Marie-Helene Bertino
Safe as Houses
Will Boast
Power Ballads
David Borofka
Hints of His Mortality
Robert Boswell
Dancing in the Movies
Mark Brazaitis
The River of Lost Voices: Stories from Guatemala
Jack Cady
The Burning and Other Stories
Pat Carr
The Women in the Mirror
Kathryn Chetkovich
Friendly Fire
Cyrus Colter
The Beach Umbrella
Marian Crotty
What Counts as Love
Jennine Capó Crucet
How to Leave Hialeah
Jennifer S. Davis
Her Kind of Want
Janet Desaulniers
What You've Been Missing
Sharon Dilworth
The Long White
Susan M. Dodd
Old Wives' Tales
Thomas A. Dodson
No Use Pretending

Merrill Feitell
Here Beneath Low-Flying Planes
Christian Felt
The Lightning Jar
James Fetler
Impossible Appetites: Nine Stories
Starkey Flythe Jr.
Lent: The Slow Fast
Kathleen Founds
When Mystical Creatures Attack!
Sohrab Homi Fracis
Ticket to Minto: Stories of India and America
H. E. Francis
The Itinerary of Beggars
Abby Frucht
Fruit of the Month
Tereze Glück
May You Live in Interesting Times
Ivy Goodman
Heart Failure
Barbara Hamby
Lester Higata's 20th Century
Edward Hamlin
Night in Erg Chebbi and Other Stories
Ann Harleman
Happiness
Elizabeth Harris
The Ant Generator
Ryan Harty
Bring Me Your Saddest Arizona
Charles Haverty
Excommunicados
Mary Hedin
Fly Away Home: Eighteen Short Stories
Beth Helms
American Wives
Jim Henry
Thank You for Being Concerned and Sensitive
Allegra Hyde
Of This New World
Bruce Johnson
Love, Dirt
Matthew Lansburgh
Outside Is the Ocean
Lisa Lenzo
Within the Lighted City
Kathryn Ma
All That Work and Still No Boys
Renée Manfredi
Where Love Leaves Us
Susan Onthank Mates
The Good Doctor
John McNally
Troublemakers
Molly McNett
One Dog Happy
Tessa Mellas
Lungs Full of Noise
Kate Milliken
If I'd Known You Were Coming

Kevin Moffett
Permanent Visitors
Lee B. Montgomery
Whose World Is This?
Rod Val Moore
Igloo among Palms
Lucia Nevai
Star Game
Thisbe Nissen
Out of the Girls' Room and into the Night
Dan O'Brien
Eminent Domain
Janice Obuchowski
The Woods
Philip F. O'Connor
Old Morals, Small Continents, Darker Times
Robert Oldshue
November Storm
Eileen O'Leary
Ancestry
Sondra Spatt Olsen
Traps
Elizabeth Oness
Articles of Faith
Lon Otto
A Nest of Hooks
Natalie L. M. Petesch
After the First Death There Is No Other
Marilène Phipps-Kettlewell
The Company of Heaven: Stories from Haiti
Glen Pourciau
Invite
C. E. Poverman
The Black Velvet Girl
Michael Pritchett
The Venus Tree
Nancy Reisman
House Fires
Josh Rolnick
Pulp and Paper
Sari Rosenblatt
Father Guards the Sheep
Blake Sanz
The Boundaries of Their Dwelling
Elizabeth Searle
My Body to You
Jennifer Sears
What Mennonite Girls Are Good For
Marguerite Sheffer
The Man in the Banana Trees
Enid Shomer
Imaginary Men
Chad Simpson
Tell Everyone I Said Hi
Heather A. Slomski
The Lovers Set Down Their Spoons
Marly Swick
A Hole in the Language
Barry Targan
Harry Belten and the Mendelssohn Violin Concerto

Annabel Thomas
The Phototropic Woman
Jim Tomlinson
Things Kept, Things Left Behind
Douglas Trevor
The Thin Tear in the Fabric of Space
Laura Valeri
The Kind of Things Saints Do
Anthony Varallo
This Day in History
Ruvanee Pietersz Vilhauer
The Water Diviner and Other Stories
Sharon Wahl
Everything Flirts: Philosophical Romances
Don Waters
Desert Gothic
Lex Williford
Macauley's Thumb
Miles Wilson
Line of Fall
Russell Working
Resurrectionists
Emily Wortman-Wunder
Not a Thing to Comfort You
Ashley Wurzbacher
Happy Like This
Charles Wyatt
Listening to Mozart
Don Zancanella
Western Electric

www.ingramcontent.com/pod-product-compliance
Lightning Source LLC
LaVergne TN
LVHW051003080826
845145LV00009B/2426

* 9 7 8 1 6 8 5 9 7 0 3 9 0 *